Rocco

by

Tracie Podger

*My dark, Man!
Love him!
Tracie x*

Copyright

Rocco

Tracie Podger

© Tracie Podger 2015

ISBN:1514749629

Cover Designer: Margreet Asselbergs

Formatted by KBK Publishing

Chapter One

The smell of lemons drifted through the evening air and a welcome breeze ruffled my hair—the heat had been consuming that day. I sat on a bench under the shade of a vine watching my mother pick the ripe lemons from a tree in the orchard. My father was walking back from tending the olive grove holding the hand of my younger sister. I loved my father, he was my hero, and the person I wanted to be. He was kind, loving and worked hard for his family. Little was I to know that would be my last happy memory of him.

My name is Rocco and this is my story.

****

My childhood had been idyllic. My brother, Enrico, my sister, Adriana, and I had acres of farmland to play in. Days were spent running around the farm getting dusty as I helped my father with the olives. We had a small farm on the outskirts of a tiny village in Campania, Italy; it's population no more than four hundred residents. Children made lifelong friends; my father often took me to meet his after a long day tending the land. The men would gather together at the local coffee shop in the evenings, sitting outside with their espresso and wine debating the price of olive oil and putting the world to rights. Many had never left the village, they had married their childhood sweetheart, watched their children grow and leave for the bright lights of a city someplace. Although they always returned. The village had a pull, there was something magical every festival time when families were reunited, generations gathered together to celebrate Saint Rocco, my namesake.

Parties were thrown in the piazza where local dishes of rabbit stew were served to all. Among the locals there would be a few tourists and they were always made welcome.

But life started to change when I was in my early teens. A family, a Mafia family had decided the residents of my village needed their protection and that came at a cost. Who we needed protection from was anyone's guess but each month a payment had to be made. I watched my father hand over his hard earned cash to thugs in smart suits and fancy cars. That payment would leave him short, meant he worked harder, longer and his happy nature started to be replaced with resentment.

"Rocco, help your father with that crate," I heard. My mother's voice had brought me out of my thoughts.

I stood and took the wooden crate from my father who straightened; his hands rubbed his lower back. He was getting old, too old to be carrying heavy crates of olives.

"Papa, where do you want this?" I asked.

"In the shed, Rocco. Tomorrow they go for pressing," he replied with a smile.

Our farm produced the most succulent olives, most were used to produce rich, virgin oil and some would be left in bowls and eaten. It was said the quality of our olives, of the lemons and fruits from our orchard came because my father would water the land from the River Sele.

I was walking back from the small wooden shed, a shed desperately in need of repair when a large black car arrived leaving a trail of dust in its wake. I saw my father push back his shoulders and stand tall. He ushered Adriana over to our mother as he waited for the occupants to exit. I walked to my father's side.

"Rocco, take your mother and Adriana inside," he whispered.

"I'll stay with you, Papa."

"Please, do as I say."

I sighed. I knew who the men were. I also knew that my father and some of his friends had decided they had paid enough and gained nothing in return. I'd heard them talk about standing together and refusing payment. It was with reluctance that I turned and walked away.

"We need to go inside," I said as I reached my mother. I could see the fearful look in her eyes and the worry lines deepen on her brow.

"Who are those men?" Adrian asked.

"No one you need to worry about. Now in," I replied.

Before we had made it to the door I heard raised voices. I spun on my heels and saw my father being dragged to the car. I ran, shouting as I did. My brother, just a couple of years older than me, had emerged from an outbuilding. He also ran to my father's aid.

"Leave him the fuck alone!" I shouted.

One of the thugs laughed and I came to an abrupt halt as I saw what he held in his hand. A gun, a small handgun was pointing at my father's head. My mother screamed, my sister cried and I looked at the terrified face of my father as he shook his head at me.

"Go inside, Rocco. This is not your fight," he said.

Before I could respond, my mother was by my side, she pulled on the thug's arm. He swiped his arm and knocked her to the floor. I had no chance to react before that gun was pointing my way. Enrico launched himself at the man. He wasn't strong enough to knock the gun from his hand and soon found himself on his backside alongside my father.

"Do as your father says. This is not your fight. Not yet anyway," I heard.

Exciting from the car was a man in a grey suit. He had a scar on his cheek, dark hair and in his hand he held a short wooden stick. He brought that stick down hard on my brother's legs. The sound of my brother's scream is one I will always remember. My body froze, my brain stilled, undecided what to do as my father and brother were dragged into the rear of the car and it roared back up the drive.

We never saw them alive again.

****

I knelt on the floor, my mother was sobbing when my uncle Geraldo came running towards the house. Adriana had been to fetch him. He gathered my mother from my arms and carried her into the house.

I paced, my hands were bunched so tight by my side that my nails drew blood. I gritted my teeth together and my jaw ached. I had never felt such anger in all my life, and guilt. A crushing guilt washed over me. I should have done something; I should have fought them regardless of the consequence. I listened to my mother's cries, to her curses and shouts. It wasn't long before people began to arrive, friends and family had gathered after hearing the news. The women took my mother to her bedroom and the men got together to talk. I was left on the outside, deemed too young to be involved. In my head I knew though, I would kill that man one day.

As I passed the kitchen I saw the men sat around the table in heated discussion. I wanted to join them, but as I made to sit, my uncle spoke.

"Take care of your sister, Rocco."

I didn't want to be excluded. I didn't want to be pushed to one side and treated like a child. I had seen my father scared. I had witnessed him being dragged into a car and I knew he would never return. I wanted revenge. I was angry, so very angry.

I slammed the door as I left the kitchen and headed back to the yard. I sat in the dark on the same bench I had sat no more than a couple of hours previous. I kept the face of my father's abductor in my mind, wanting to memorise every little bit of him. I wanted it imprinted in my brain so every time I closed my eyes his face was all I saw.

"One day, I'll come for you," I whispered.

It was a couple of hours later that the men started to leave; my uncle joined me on that bench. At first we sat in silence with just a pat on my leg as a way of comfort from him.

"I'm sorry," he said. "This was my idea. I talked your father into joining us. I had no idea he would be the first they came for."

"You find their bodies and you bring them home," I replied.

Geraldo nodded. His body slumped and I placed my arm around his shoulders as he sobbed. I was yet to cry, no tears would leave my eyes. I would not grieve until I had sought revenge, until that man had paid a price for his actions.

"You have to take on the farm, Rocco. Your mother is going to need you. Get those thoughts out of your head. We did wrong, we thought we could stand up to them as a group and look what happened. You can't avenge your father on your own," Geraldo said.

How he knew what was going through my head, I had no idea. But he was wrong.

****

It was two days later that my father's body was found. He was placed in a sitting position in a ditch but on full view of the one road that led in and out of the village. It was a warning. He was used as a message to those that wanted to defy—this is what happens to those that do.

His body was brought home and he was laid to rest a week later. There was no investigation, very little police involvement. A robbery, they had concluded. I wasn't dumb enough to know they had no choice but to record that verdict, no doubt they worked for the *family*. We never found Enrico.

The whole village attended Papa's funeral. It was a blistering day and dressed in my black suit I was one of six who carried his coffin through the cobbled streets and to the church. Sweat ran down my back soaking my white shirt. Geraldo helped my mother, Adriana was to her side as they followed behind; she stumbled a little, her grief making her legs unsteady.

It was after the service as we filed out of the church that I saw him. That same black car was parked on the side of the road; he was leaning against the rear door. I stopped and looked at him. He stared back. I might have been young, but he knew what I was thinking. He smirked at me before throwing his cigarette to the ground and casually climbed back in his car.

"Keep moving," I heard. My sister had arrived at my side. She had witnessed the brief exchange of silent communication.

Adriana placed her arm through mine and we followed the party back to the piazza.

"Please, Rocco, don't do anything," she whispered.

"I can't promise you anything. I'm sorry," I replied.

"Think of Mamma, of me. We can't lose you too."

"You're not going to lose me. Now, let's get this over with."

I always thought it strange to hear laughter at a wake. I wanted people to mourn, to cry, to feel the rage inside that I did and to scream and shout. I wanted the sun to stop shining, for the birds to stop singing. Why should the world go on when I had just buried my father? Why should people be happy when my brother had no final resting place?

Needing to be alone, I left the wake. I left my mother in the care of Geraldo and her sister, Elvira, and I made my way home.

I shrugged off my jacket and undid my black tie, pulling it through the collar of my shirt as I walked. Rolling it into a ball, I stuffed it in the pocket of my trousers. Arriving home I changed into jeans, deciding to go shirtless, and set about to do all the jobs my father had planned but never managed. First on the list was repair of his storage shed.

As the sun beat down, I nailed new planks of wood to the roof; I repaired the broken door and replaced the glass in the window. Sweat rolled from my brow and blisters formed on my hands. My skin glistened, coated with a sheen of perspiration. I worked hard all day and into the evening.

"Rocco." I heard my name being called from the house.

Packing up the tools and leaving them in the shed, I made my way to the house. My mother and her sister were sat in the kitchen. She looked up as I entered and held out her arms for me. I took a seat beside her, pulling her into a hug.

"Where have you been?" she asked.

"Working. I needed to work."

"You need to eat. Let me fix something for you."

"Mamma, you buried your husband today. Let us look after you."

By *us,* I meant Adriana and Elvira. No man was getting close to the counter tops in that kitchen. They busied themselves preparing figs and meats, cheese and olives, which they placed on the kitchen table. A carafe of red wine was set down in the centre with four small tumblers and we drank a toast to my father while we ate.

Chapter Two

Day after day I toiled the land, I fixed the house and the outbuildings. I worked like a horse. I noticed my body change, develop. Muscles were defined across my shoulders, down my arms and stomach. I needed to work to forget and to build my strength for the day I would need it.

We needed supplies and Geraldo had borrowed a car to take us to the city. It was an hour drive and something we did once a month. Most of what we ate we either grew, bought from neighbours or the small local shops in the village, the same local shops that bought our produce.

As a child I always enjoyed the family day out. Two families would pile into the beaten up truck my father owned, the kids generally in the back and hanging on for dear life as Papa cornered too fast. There wasn't the need for much driving in the village, other than to take the crates of olives to the press.

We parked and each went their separate ways. Sandwiched between the hardware store and a butchers was a small glass fronted shop, a shop I hadn't seen before. Its windows were dark but the sign caught my eye. I smiled as I entered. The smell of antiseptic hit my nose and the most decorated person I'd ever seen greeted me.

"What can I do for you?" he asked.

"I want a tattoo," I replied. Until that moment I had never wanted a tattoo.

"Any idea what kind of tattoo?"

"No, do you have any designs I can look at?"

He handed me a folder of photographs, each image was of a body part and the most amazing tattoos. I stopped flicking at an ornate dragon snaking up the arm of a guy.

"You won't get that done in one sitting, unless you've got a few hours to spare," he said, looking over my shoulder.

"I have a few hours but I want something added to it."

I settled into the chair and looked at the clock on the wall. I had the whole day to spare. The supplies I wanted could wait if needs be and the rest of the family would take the day to shop, lunch and catch up with friends.

Three hours later I looked at the dragon. More importantly, I looked at the words written underneath.

Strength and Courage

That dragon snaked up my arm, its head coming to rest on my shoulder as if looking at me. Piercing eyes stared at mine—it was perfect.

With instructions on after-care given, I pulled on my shirt, paid and left. The tattoo had taken most of my money but I'd make that back. I had started to do odd jobs for the neighbours, the elderly ones that were unable to keep up with the maintenance of their farms. I was earning enough to provide for the family with a little spare for me.

"Where have you been all day?" Adriana asked as I met her back at the car.

I lit a cigarette before I answered.

"And when did you start to smoke?" she added.

"Nowhere and none of your business. Where have you been or more importantly, who have you been with?" I asked.

I had heard a rumour that she had a friend, a boyfriend of sorts and I wanted to know more. She was too young to be out with boys unaccompanied.

"Nowhere and none of your business," she answered with a smile.

"I will find out and if he's no good, you'll stop seeing him."

"Oh, Rocco. You're not my father," she protested.

"I am head of this family, just warning you."

The months that had followed my father's death had been hard. We were all still adjusting and I had ignored Adriana sneaking out at night, allowing her a little freedom because I felt she needed it. However, it was time for that to stop. Her safety was more important than her freedom.

Although the thugs no longer visited our house, I knew my uncle paid the hefty sum required to ensure they stayed away. I also knew he was struggling to do that.

****

Geraldo joined us for dinner; his wife had passed away in childbirth, both her and the son they were to have gone in a heartbeat. He never remarried, he looked after his farm on his own and he was getting old. It was a struggle for him.

After dinner, as was customary, Geraldo and I moved to the yard. We sat at the small wooden table with our wine and cigarettes.

"Rocco, you're a man now, you need to find a good woman to look after you," he said.

I shook my head. I had no need for a good woman, it was the bad ones I had recently discovered—they were the ones I liked at that point in my life.

"I see you, you sow your oats, and all men should before they settle down. I know your mother is concerned for you. You work all day and, shall we say, party all night. It's not healthy."

For the past couple of weeks I had left the house each evening, met with friends in the piazza for wine and ended up in a back alley with any woman I could. I fucked—I fucked a lot. It was fun to see how many women I could have. My friends mocked me, jealous of course because they couldn't compete.

"I have no desire to settle down, Geraldo. There's no one in the village I'd want to marry," I said.

"This village, this life, it stifles you doesn't it?"

I was surprised by his comment.

"No, I just have things to do before I settle down with anyone."

"Do those *things* involve your father, your brother?"

"Yes, I made a promise to myself and I will keep that promise."

"And you will get yourself killed keeping that promise. Is that what you want?"

Somewhere in the back of my mind I knew I would never settle down until I had killed the man who had destroyed my family. I would never get close to anyone for fear of them being hurt. The want for revenge ate me up inside like a cancer. It was all I thought of before I slept, it was all I dreamt about and all I imagined when I woke. Images of that man at my feet, blood pooling around his head, his eyes staring up at me as he took his last breath were what kept me in the village. Yes I was stifled, not by village life, but by my burning desire to murder.

It was two months later that I got my wish, that the burning desire was achieved.

Adriana had decided to accompany me one evening. I hadn't wanted her to. My evenings were generally spent with my friends, men only sitting at the café enjoying our time after a long hard day on our respective farms.

I saw him walk across the piazza, strolling without a care in the world. It had been a few years since I had last seen him but time had not diminished his face from my memory. It was the scar that ran down his cheek that I focused on. I held my breath. Perhaps he had sensed someone staring at him as he turned and looked my way. There was no recognition in his eyes, maybe just a flicker of something but he scowled and carried on walking.

"Stay here," I said to Adriana as I stood.

"Where are you going?"

"Just stay here. Go on home if I'm not back in ten minutes, you hear?"

"Rocco, why can't I come with you?"

"Because I said you can't. Now do as you're told for once," I snapped.

I followed him at a distance. He stopped a couple of times to greet people, ever the gentleman. But the faces of the people he stopped to speak to didn't always return the smile he gave. He wasn't liked. It was a short walk before he turned towards a small stone house. I was surprised. For someone who wore the finest clothes, who had the largest car, I wasn't expecting him to live in such a modest house. I guessed it wasn't his home when I saw him knock on the door. A young woman opened it, young enough to be his daughter; she didn't smile as she let him in.

I crept to the window; I had no plan and no idea of what I was going to do. I just wanted to see what he was doing there. The young woman was crying, he was shouting, calling her a whore and then he slapped her face. She fell to the floor just as I stepped on something. The crack of a broken branch echoed and I ducked down, out of sight. A minute passed before I moved. With my back to the wall of the house, I made my way around the side, into the yard and a small orchard. I was aiming for the back of the house and as I rounded the last corner, I came face to face with him.

"What the fuck do you think you're doing?" he asked.

He had leant against the wall smoking his cigarette. I stood tall.

"I know you, don't I?" he added.

"Yes, you killed my father, my brother," I replied.

He looked at me for a moment before laughing. "You're the skinny kid from the farm. Well, you certainly changed over the years."

The young woman leaving the house momentarily distracted me; he took that moment to attack. He lunged forward, grabbing me by the front of my shirt with one hand, his other arm pulled back ready to punch. I got in first. I punched as hard as I could to his stomach, forcing the air from his lungs. He bent slightly at the waist trying to catch his breath but he never let go of my shirt. I twisted, hearing it tear as I tried to move away from him. I punched, he punched, and a blow to the side of my head rocked me on my feet. The girl screamed as she pulled on his arm. He had to let go of me then, he used his arm to knock her to the ground. That very act took me back years, it was the same thing he had done to my mother. Rage took over. I focused solely on him and we fought.

He was panting, out of breath, but I knew he would never let me walk away alive. I had to kill him and all I had were my fists. He was larger than me, stronger, but I had youth on my side and I was fitter. He pushed me away and for a moment we were separated. It was then that the woman ran back from the house. I hadn't noticed her leave. She held a large kitchen knife in her hand. We stood watching her, she was sobbing and her body was shaking but her focus was on him not me.

"Fucking do it," he snarled at her before laughing.

"Go on! Fucking do it!" he shouted again before taking a step towards her.

She backed off, moving more to my side. She was never going to stab him, but whatever was going through her mind, she needed help. Neither of us would live to see the morning if nothing was done. I took the knife from her hand and lunged at him. He wasn't expecting that. The knife entered his side and I pushed it in as far as I could. His eyes were wide with shock and his hands covered mine trying to pull the knife out.

Eventually he fell to his knees. He wheezed, bloody foam ran from his mouth and blood ran down his side. I looked him straight in the eye and smiled as I watched him take his last breath. He fell forwards, face first in the dirt at my feet.

I don't know how long passed. It may have been minutes; it may have been seconds, before the woman started to scream.

"You killed him," she shouted.

I looked at her stunned.

"You're the one who came out with the knife, you wanted to kill him too," I replied.

"Oh, God, you killed him." She knelt beside him, holding his head in her hands and crying. "Someone, help," she cried out.

I stumbled backwards, not expecting that, before turning and running. I ran all the way home.

****

My mother was in the kitchen as I crashed through the door. She dropped a glass she was holding in shock at the sight of me I guessed. I looked down. My hands were covered in his blood and the front of my shirt was torn. I rushed to the sink scrubbing the skin and watching the water run red.

"What did you do?" she whispered.

"I killed him, like I promised myself I would," I replied.

"They'll come for you, Rocco. Oh, my son, I can't lose you too."

"And I'll be waiting, Mamma. I'll be waiting for them."

"You're one man. What do you think you will be able to do?" The anguish in her voice was evident.

"The villages can stand side by side. For once, we can all stand together and fight."

"Rocco, the villagers are old men, the young one's don't care enough to stand by you. I need to speak to Geraldo. We need to get you away from here."

She called for Adriana and sent her to fetch my uncle.

I pulled the shirt over my head and threw it in the bin just as my mother returned.

"Geraldo is on his way," she said.

I nodded before pouring myself a tumbler of wine and sitting at the kitchen table. As the adrenalin wore off so reality set in. My mother was right; the villagers were too old to stand against the family, too scared to fight. Some of my friends, over the past couple of years, had joined the family opting for the money and the smart clothes.

My mother came and sat by my side, she placed her hand on my arm, and her fingers traced the tattoo of the dragon.

"I'm proud of you," she said quietly. "But now you have to leave."

"I can't leave you with all this," I said, indicating with my head towards the orchard and farm.

"I managed it before and I'll manage it again. I want you to have a life, Rocco, and leaving here is the only way that's going to happen."

We heard tyres screech to a halt on the dirt drive outside. My mother stood to look through the window. She relaxed as Geraldo came through the door.

"So you did it then?" he said as he sat. I nodded.

"You know they will come after you. They can't let this go unpunished. The first place they will look is here so we need to get you away."

"I guess I can head for Rome or the city," I replied.

"I was thinking further than that. I have a friend, Rocco, an old friend who lives in America. I called him; he's willing to have you there. You'll be safe with him but there is one thing…"

He paused as he took a sip of the wine my mother had poured for him.

"He has his own *family*, in Washington, DC."

"So, I kill a man from the Cosa Nostra and you send me to another?"

"It's the safest place, Rocco. Guiseppi is old school. You remember him, Dina?"

"I do. Rocco, he's a good man. You'll be safe and that's all I care about," my mother replied.

So it was decided. I was to leave the village, leave Italy, and head to America. I didn't own a passport but was told not to worry about that. I then began to wonder who my uncle really was. He had connected friends, he could get me a passport and he could send me to America on a moments notice. I left my uncle and mother to their discussion and headed for my bedroom.

The room was sparsely furnished; there was no need for elaborate décor or furniture. We lived simply and that suited me. I pulled an old suitcase from the top of a wardrobe and began to fill it with the small amount of clothes I owned. In my mind I believed I would return one day.

It took three days for a passport to be delivered to Geraldo. Those three days I'd spent moving from farm to farm in the village, hiding out in sheds and outbuildings. No one wanted me in their home for fear of being punished. On the fourth day, dirty and scared, I was driven to the airport. I had some dollars in my pocket; I didn't question where the money had come from. Geraldo drove and with the window down, I watched my beloved Italian landscape pass me by.

****

The flight was long and cramped, made marginally better by the striking brunette giving me sly looks and shy smiles whenever I caught her. She was sitting across the aisle from me. I could speak English, of course. We were taught a universal language in school but my accent was heavy. Most people found it hard to understand me.

"Going on holiday?" she asked.

"Something like that," I replied.

"I've been on a tour around Italy, amazing country," she drew out the word 'amazing'.

She then spent the next hour detailing every part of her holiday, the sights she had seen, the food she had eaten, and the Italian men she had dated. She began to bore me. She was crass and I prayed not all American women would be the same. She was nice to look at but her accent grated on me. Maybe I was just cranky from the journey. I was tired and already missing home.

When the plane landed, I took my time unbuckling my seat belt. I deliberately held back letting her exit before me. I had no desire to spend any more time with her than necessary. Dulles Airport was about the busiest place I had ever been to. I was on edge though; the passport I was carrying was a fake. I had to pretend I was on holiday, a two-week break to catch up with family and friends.

After scrutinising my passport, I was free to proceed to the luggage claim. I spotted the brunette and decided she may actually be of use so stood beside her.

"Oh, I thought you'd already got through," she said, smiling up at me.

"Need my case first."

"Oh, yeah," she said with a laugh.

Dumb bitch, I thought.

"You want to get a coffee before you head off on your travels?" she asked.

"Sure, why not."

She reached forward to lift her suitcase from the belt, being the gentleman that I was; I placed my hand on her arm stopping her before grabbing it myself. A minute later I located my own bag and loaded them both onto a trolley. She would make a convenient companion to walk through security with.

Once through, I paused, searching the faces in the crowd waiting to meet friends and loved ones. As I scanned I came to rest on a man, he nodded as he approached.

I had never seen him before but had been told that someone would be at the airport to meet me; he would have seen my photograph so Geraldo had explained.

"Rocco?" he asked. I nodded.

"Time to leave, sweetheart. Nice to have met you," I said to the brunette before grabbing my case and following.

I was gone before she realised and could respond.

"Welcome to America. My names Jonathan," he said as we walked to a silver car. "How was your flight?"

"Long," I replied with a laugh.

"Guiseppi is expecting you at his house until we know what to do with you," he said with a smile.

I liked him immediately. He was older than me but not by much I guessed. A driver exited the car parked right out front and opened the boot. He took my case and I slid into the rear seat. Jonathan pointed out some landmarks as we made our way from the airport. I was aware that it was idle chitchat on the journey and the one time I broached the subject of Guiseppi, Jonathan glanced at the driver before changing the subject.

We pulled onto the drive of a large house and I was surprised at the lack of security. I imagined Guiseppi to live behind high walls and iron gates with security patrolling the grounds. Instead we were met by the man himself at the front door.

"Rocco, welcome, welcome," he said as he pulled me into an embrace.

"Thank you, and thank you for allowing me to stay," I replied.

"Come on in. Paulo, take Rocco's bag upstairs. You know which room."

I followed Guiseppi into his home, into a large kitchen where he introduced me to his family.

"Rocco, this is my wife Maria, my daughter Maria and that little one is Joey. Evelyn is out, you'll meet her later."

I smiled at the young Maria who lowered her head and rushed from the room. Joey hid behind his mother's legs.

"It's a pleasure to meet you and thank you for having me in your home," I said to Maria. I was aware of her forced smile.

"Sit, Rocco. Can I make you coffee?" she asked.

I took a seat at the kitchen table and Guiseppi sat opposite me, Jonathan to the side.

"Now, tell me. How is your uncle? I knew your father too and I'm sorry for your loss."

"Geraldo sends his regards. He spoke highly of you."

"How is your poor mother coping?" Maria asked as she placed the coffee on the table.

"She's well, she has her family to help with the farm for the time being."

I noticed Guiseppi look towards his wife; he gave her a smile and a nod of his head. She left the kitchen on what I guessed was his instruction.

"Now, tell me what happened," he said.

I started at the beginning, I wasn't sure how much Geraldo would have told him. He sat, nodded occasionally, stopped me to ask a question but mainly listened. When I had finished he turned to Jonathan.

"Find out what you can," he said. Jonathan stood and left the room.

"You did the right thing. Always, Rocco, always avenge your family. I will ensure your mother, your uncle and your sister are safe. They'll have no trouble from now on."

This gentle man, or so he appeared at first glance, sitting in front of me had morphed into something far more frightening and I was reminded of who he was. His features were hard; his dark brown eyes stared straight at me. However, a voice from the hallway completely changed him.

"Papa? I'm home."

The most beautiful girl I'd ever seen walked into the kitchen, stopping abruptly when she saw me. Her cheeks coloured as she looked from me to her father.

"Ah, Evelyn, perfect timing. Come, meet Rocco. He's staying with us for a while. Rocco, my bella, my daughter, Evelyn."

She looked to the floor, obviously shy, and I took the opportunity to study her. Her long brown hair curled around her face, around her shoulders and was so glossy. When she did look up, her hazel eyes met mine. She was breath taking and she was young. Way younger than she looked I imagined. I stood and held out my hand.

"Pleased to meet you, Evelyn."

Her small hand enclosed around mine, she mumbled before rushing from the room.

"Always so shy. Always so clumsy too," Guiseppi laughed. "Now, you must be exhausted. Let me show you to your room. You can rest and we'll meet for dinner at eight."

I followed him up two flights of stairs to a row of identical white doors lining a corridor. Guiseppi pointed out a bathroom and then headed to the last room. He opened the door and stood to one side, allowing me to enter.

He nodded before closing the door and leaving me in my new bedroom. My case had been laid on the bed and I opened it, removed clothes and hung them in the wardrobe. There was a wooden chest of drawers under the window, a single bed and a bedside cabinet. A selection of towels had been placed at the end of the bed and I moved them to the floor. Kicking off my shoes and taking my shirt off, I lay down and linked my hands behind my head. I stared at the white painted ceiling and at the decorative moulding surrounding the light fitting. There was nothing opulent about the house, it was understated but classy. The furniture was solid and well built, the bed was comfortable—that comfortable that I soon found myself drifting off.

I was woken by a knock on the door. It took me a moment to get my bearings and I was disorientated. There was a second knock. I swung my legs to the floor and headed for the door. I opened it to see Evelyn.

Her eyes were fixed on my stomach and I glanced down to see what had caught her attention. Her cheeks coloured a flaming red that had crept from her neck. She mumbled something about dinner before rushing away. I was bemused.

I pulled the shirt back over my head before making my way down to the kitchen and joining the family for dinner.

"Tell us about your family, Rocco," Maria asked as we settled down to eat.

There were many people both her and Guiseppi knew from the village and I soon realised it had been their home many years ago too.

Neither Evelyn nor Maria spoke the whole time we ate. I noticed the odd glance from Evelyn but mostly she kept her face down. Joey bounced around, a bundle of energy and wore his mother out.

Chapter Three

I was given a couple of days to settle in, to acclimatise to the time difference before being called into Guiseppi's office. He was sat at a large desk, Jonathan to one side.

"Rocco, your uncle told of you of my business I take it?" he said.

"He did. He believed being with you would be the safest place for me."

"And he's correct. Let me explain how we work. Jonathan is my Consigliere, he advises. Paulo and Ricardo are Caporegime, let's call them head of departments," he chuckled as he spoke.

"Joe runs a tight ship here, Rocco. There are no hard drugs on our streets and there is no protection money paid. If a business wants a dispute settled all parties are brought before us and if the dispute is settled, a donation is always welcome. That donation goes to the church. We don't work the way other families do. Joe looks after this neighbourhood and they respect him for it. However, fall outside the *rules* and a price is paid," Jonathan added.

"How do you earn your money, if that's not too bold a question?" I asked.

Joe, as I was now allowed to call him, laughed. "Rocco, my boy, import of course. We import some of the finest goods from Italy and sell it to the local stores. We *acquire* goods, which are sold to the local residents. I believe in them having the opportunity to buy items they couldn't necessarily afford."

I guessed the import part of his business wasn't declared to the taxman, and the acquisition of goods probably not legal either.

"You need to work, Rocco. Every man needs to earn his way and have money in his pocket to spend on wine and women. So you'll work with me."

There was no invitation to refuse his offer and so started my career with Guiseppi Morietti, local gangland boss, Cosa Nostra or, as the press called them, the Mafia.

****

I spent the next couple of months shadowing Joe, listening and learning. He was very well respected by the locals, they made a point of stopping and chatting to him, shaking his hand and offering goods from their stores. He smiled and greeted each and every one, often by name. He introduced me to everyone he met.

"Always respect these people, Rocco. Without them we would have no business," he said as we walked through Columbia Heights.

Two guys, two very large guys who walked a few paces behind, always accompanied him. Perhaps the streets of DC were not as safe as he would have me believe.

I enjoyed working with Joe, with the guys he surrounded himself with and it wasn't long before I was in a fortunate position. I took orders from Joe and I handed those orders down the line. There was only one problem I had no idea how to solve—Evelyn.

It had become obvious over the past months that she liked me, whether it was teenage infatuation or more, I wasn't sure.

I'd been helping unload a lorry of *acquired* goods the previous evening and slept in late. It was as I finished my shower that I realised I had left my clothes in the bedroom. With just a towel around my waist I made my way to my bedroom. The door was ajar and knowing I had closed it before I left, I quietly pushed it open. Evelyn had her back to me and a t-shirt of mine raised to her face. I tried to back out, not wanting her to know I had seen for fear of causing her embarrassment but a creaky floorboard had her spin on her heels.

I watched the usual blush creep up her neck and into her cheeks. She stared at the floor, mumbling about collecting washing. I was flattered by her attention. I also knew she was too young and my security, my family's safety, depended on her father. I was under no illusion that her father would go ballistic should he find out his daughter had feelings for me.

"Thank you, Evelyn. I took care of it myself," I said.

She quickly pushed past me, not giving me time to move out the way. Her body was close to mine and I inhaled her scent. I closed my eyes briefly as she assaulted my senses.

****

Evelyn did everything she could to avoid me over the next couple of months and I was pleased with that. At meal times she would sit in silence, staying out of the conversation as much as possible. There was a change in atmosphere and I knew her mother was aware; I overheard them talking one evening.

"He's no good for you, Evelyn," Maria said.

I had retired to the back yard for a cigarette. It was a muggy evening and the kitchen window was open allowing the conversation to flow out to where I sat.

"I love your Papa with all my heart, but this isn't a life I want for you," she added.

"I don't know what you mean," Evelyn replied.

"You do, my sweet girl. Be careful who you give your heart to, that one will break it. He's too old, too damaged already."

It saddened me to hear Maria speak that way. Yes, I was too old, I knew that and it was for that reason I would never take advantage of Evelyn but was I damaged? I wanted nothing more than to fall in love and marry, to have children with someone who loved me back. I ground the cigarette in the ashtray and stood. As I did, Maria made her way into the yard. She stopped abruptly, surprised to see me I guessed. I nodded and gave her a small smile before making my way back into the house. I had work to do that evening, a problem to solve. I also knew it was time to find somewhere to live. I had outstayed my welcome and it would be easier to avoid Evelyn if I wasn't sleeping in a bedroom opposite hers.

****

Life changed a month or so later. Maria got cancer; it ate away at her at such speed. She had been poorly for a few weeks, often sitting on her own wrapped in a blanket in the sweltering garden room. Evelyn seemed to have taken over looking after the family. She cooked, cleaned and kept busy. Joe was distraught. He took a step back from business to care for Maria, and I took a step up and conducted his affairs in his absence.

I avoided going to the house as much as possible, not for any reason other than to give the family some privacy. I stayed at the hotel most nights. However, one evening I needed to speak to Joe. I opened the front door and called out. There was no answer. As I made my way to the kitchen I heard my name being called. Maria was in her usual position on the small sofa in the garden room.

"Maria, is there anything I can get for you?" I asked.

"Sit with me for a moment. Joe is in the garden with Evelyn, he's teaching her how to tend to my flowers. I don't know why. They are lovely but they don't mean that much," she winced as she moved into a sitting position.

"It's a dumb question to ask how you're feeling I guess," I replied.

Maria chuckled before giving me a smile.

"Evelyn is in love you with, you know that, right?"

I nodded my head. "I promise you, Maria, I would never take advantage of your daughter."

"I want to ask one thing of you. Don't ever put her in danger. She is a kind young woman. I want her to fall in love and be happy, to marry and have children; and to have a future, a *safe* future."

After nodding, I stood and left. My chat with Joe could wait and I headed for my car. I didn't believe Maria had given her blessing, she was telling me that I couldn't offer that *safe future*.

It was late one night that Maria passed away with her family by her side.

I kept out of the way as much as possible, allowing the family time to grieve. It was at the funeral that something inside me changed. I watched Evelyn support her father, her sister and brother. I watched her conduct herself in such a refined manner; she was a grown woman and a knot formed in my stomach when I watched her. She was even more beautiful in grief than normal. But, no matter what that knot meant, she would never be available to me. I wasn't good enough for her.

****

Joe found me a house, a small one in need of some repair but in a good location. He owned it, and I set about making it my home. I had no furniture but I had started to earn well and, of course, I received either donations or discounts from the stores I bought items from.

"It's looking good," Joe said when he visited one day.

"I used to repair the farm back home."

I had repainted the living room and kitchen, fixed the cupboards and polished the wooden floor.

"I want you to keep the key to the house, you may need it. Now, we have some trouble to deal with."

A local drug gang had been trying to muscle in; Joe allowed the sale of dope but nothing more. This gang had decided they might try their luck with something stronger and it was time to show them the error of their ways. Drugs were not something I was interested in; my choice of high had become the women that threw themselves at me.

I took Paulo and a new guy, Mack, with me. Mack had recently joined the gym Joe owned; he was a fighter, a fucking good fighter. It didn't take long to find the person I was after, he was stood at the corner of a block waiting for a customer I guessed. Paulo drove, Mack was upfront and I sat in the back of the black Mercedes. We pulled alongside; Mack got out and opened the rear door. The dealer was *encouraged* to join me.

"José, I'm glad we've caught up with you," I said.

It was very clear he was uncomfortable. He knew our rules, he knew he had broken them and he also knew this wasn't a social call.

"Where are we going?" he asked.

"For a drive. It's a nice evening for a drive, don't you think?"

I took pleasure in watching his hands shake. I knew then what those old friends back in the village felt. I had come from nothing and now I was someone to respect, to fear—I enjoyed that.

We arrived at a small bistro nestled between a deli and a barber. I liked the area, Great Falls was rural and the bistro was somewhere I visited frequently. I watched José relax; I guess he thought he was being taken for dinner. He was, except he hadn't realised he was the one on the menu.

"Get out," I said as Paulo opened the rear door for me.

I straightened my jacket before nodding to the owner, Fredrico. He had risen from his usual place at a metal table outside the front entrance.

"Rocco, it's good to see you. You're usual?" he said, his eyes darted from me to José.

"Of course," I replied. He nodded.

We followed Fredrico through the restaurant, it wasn't busy but the patrons that were there averted their gaze. We continued to walk until we reached the kitchen and then on through the rear door to a yard behind. Our dealer had started to falter. Mack gave him a shove, encouraging him to keep walking. As we did, I unbuttoned my jacket and shrugged it from my shoulders.

I spun around quick, pulled back my fist and punched the guy straight in the face. He fell to his knees. I punched him to the side of his head, anywhere I could. Blood spattered over my t-shirt, it ran through my fingers as his nose gave way and as his teeth were knocked from their sockets. He tried to protect himself as best he could.

"Why are you here?" I asked him, taking a breather from his punishment.

"I don't know," he said, his voice gurgled in his throat.

I kicked him hard, connecting with his side. "Wrong answer."

"I'll leave, I'll move on," he whimpered.

"Another wrong answer," I said.

"What the fuck do you want me to say?" he tried to shout but hadn't quite caught his breath from the kick.

I leant down and grabbed his hair, raising his face close to mine. "*Thank you for killing me quickly* should be the words you speak."

His eyes widened in fear, I let go of his head and took a step back. He didn't see the gun that Mack held, he didn't feel it press against the back of his head and I guess he wouldn't have heard the muffled shot as the bullet flew through the chamber, down the barrel and out the silencer. I jumped back as a piece of stone ricocheted where the bullet exited his head and caught me on my cheek.

"You could have fucking shot me," I said, feeling a slight sting on my cheek.

Mack laughed. "No, I aimed down. It's only a graze."

I shook my head and we made our way around the side of the restaurant and to the car. I didn't want to be visible for any length of time so avoided washing my hands in the kitchen or the restroom. Fredrico would deal with the body; he had a nice way of cleaning up after us. He liked to feed the stray dogs out back and the dealer would provide plenty of meals. We headed back to Joe's.

****

It was late by the time we arrived and the house was dark, Joe had obviously retired for the night. I had been hoping Joe would still be up, he would want to know what happened that evening. I decided to clean up, stay the night so I could chat with him in the morning. Without turning on the light I stumbled up the stairs and headed to the bathroom.

"Shit," I whispered as I banged my shoulder on the frame of the door.

I ran the taps and held my hands under the cool water; the skin on my knuckles was broken. I heard the creak of a footstep on the floorboard and looked up into the mirror. Evelyn was standing at the door.

We didn't speak as she walked towards me. She took a washcloth and held it under the water. She raised it to my cheek, holding it over the graze. The control I had exerted inside for so long gave way to an overwhelming desire for her. It had been two years that I had watched her grow into a woman, two years of holding back, of knowing she wanted me and resisting her.

I closed my eyes and sighed. I turned and took a step towards her. I rested my forehead on hers as she bunched my shirt in her hands. It wasn't a conscious movement but my hand snaked around her waist, gripping the t-shirt she was wearing. Her smell was intoxicating and my senses spiralled out of control. I nuzzled into her neck; her warm skin met my lips. My tongue trailed a path across her jawbone finding her mouth. She welcomed me in. As our kiss deepened I walked her backwards, pressing her against the wall. I needed the wall for support. And then I heard a small moan, a moan of pleasure.

"Fuck, fuck, fuck," I said as I moved away from her.

"Rocco?" she whispered.

I paced, I had just gone against everything I said I wouldn't do. I would not touch her—I wasn't worthy of her. I saw the tears that pooled in her eyes and felt like a complete shit. She rushed to the door. I needed to speak, to say something and apologise. I blocked her way.

"Let me pass, Rocco," she whispered.

"Ev, I'm sorry. I shouldn't have done that. I'm so sorry."

She ducked under my arm and as quietly as she could, she ran to her room. I stood for a moment, my head bowed and my eyes closed. I had hurt her and that was the one thing I'd never wanted to do.

As I walked to the bedroom I once slept in, I paused outside her door. I could hear her sobs. It took all my strength not to open that door, not to pull her into my arms and to kiss her again. She did something to me, something unwelcomed. She had no idea who I was or what I had done. She had no idea I was only alive because her father gave me sanctuary. I believed I would be sent packing if he thought there was even the slightest inappropriate behaviour with his daughter. I was torn. The safety of my family weighed heavily on my mind.

****

I didn't sleep at all; I tossed and turned. I dreamt of her, the smell of her skin lingered. I tasted her still and my lips tingled at the thought of crushing on hers. My cock painfully stiffened and no amount of stroking gave me the release I needed. I wanted to fuck her; I wanted to make love to her.

The following morning, with a fuzzy brain from lack of sleep, I headed to the bathroom. I wanted to be showered and out of the way before she rose. I wasn't thinking when I opened the door and walked into the hot steamy room. Evelyn was in the shower, her perfect body an outline against the tinted glass cubicle. I watched as her hands slid down her stomach to that one place I wanted to bury my face. I swallowed hard and my breathing became shallower. Perhaps she had sensed my presence as she startled and her hand flew to her mouth to stifle a scream.

She made no attempt to cover herself; instead she opened the cubicle door slightly.

"Pass me the towel please," she said.

I took the towel from the rack and handed it to her. She wrapped it around herself before stepping out. Wet hair stuck to the side of her face and droplets of water ran down her chest. I wanted to lick those droplets from her body. As she walked past, I couldn't stop myself. I reached out and held her arm; I smoothed a piece of hair from her face.

"Soon," I whispered.

She looked at me, those hazel eyes so full of trust and love. I knew then, no matter what, I had to find a way to be with her.

Chapter Four

Maybe I was over-thinking but it seemed that Joe kept me away from the house, he kept me busy. He needed to fly to New York, the Commission was meeting and he was expected to attend. The Commission was a collection of heads of prominent families and Joe was the one who often chaired, who mediated when business got strained between them. It was a long day, driving the few hours it took there and back. It gave me the chance to catch up with Joe. I told him of the dealer and how we had removed him from our streets. I got him up to speed on his various businesses in the city and any problems I had solved before he needed to become involved.

Talk soon moved onto his family.

"I worry for Evelyn," he said.

"In what way?"

"I want her to meet a nice man, a lawyer or a doctor. Someone respectable who can treat her well, give her a nice house and clothes."

I didn't answer. Maybe that was his way of telling me I was no good, just as Maria had all those years ago.

"I'm sure when she's ready she'll meet the man worthy of her," I said.

Joe rarely spoke of his other daughter, Maria, someone who was clearly unwell. She never left the house, her bedroom even. Jonathan had found a housekeeper to take the pressure off Evelyn and I knew she wanted to work.

"You know Mark Philips is looking for someone to help."

Mark Philips had been installed in one of Joe's import businesses. He was trusted but chaotic. Olive oil, some from my family farm, was just one item that found it's way into the warehouse and then onto the stores locally. Although the storeowners had a choice, the ones that owned their own stores of course, they were encouraged to purchase from Joe. He offered a fair price for his goods but that import business covered up a multitude of sins. Liquor and cigarettes were smuggled through, mixed in with the crates of oil and I knew my uncle was involved somehow.

Not that it was really any of my business but I wanted some control over where Evelyn worked. She was headstrong but I felt a sense of duty to make sure she was safe and Philips was the ideal choice. Thankfully it didn't take a great deal of manipulation before Joe sent Evelyn to meet Philips.

****

One evening I had sat with Joe in the kitchen, I heard Evelyn call out as she returned home. I hadn't seen her in over a week. She stumbled as she came through the door, unsure at first how to behave around me. As usual her cheeks coloured as her father invited her to sit and tell us about her day. It had been her first day at work and I was pleased to see the animation in her face as she recounted her day.

I passed her a coffee, as our hands brushed against each other I felt a surge of static pulse up my arm and my heart quickened. She pulled away quickly, drank her coffee and left.

"Rocco, I want you to stay here. I hear rumours friends of José, the dealer, are not happy with his *disappearance*. I want to know my family will be safe," Joe said.

"Of course and you'll have no trouble with them, I'll make sure of that."

Joe was leaving on another trip to New York the following day and I was pleased that he was to leave me in charge. I wasn't sure I wanted to be too far away from Evelyn. I had promised her 'soon' yet had no idea what that meant. I made a decision to discuss the situation with Jonathan.

"Rocco, you have a call," I heard.

I made my way to Joe's office and Jonathan handed me the telephone.

"Rocco," I said.

"Hey, it's me, Adriana. Geraldo has bought me a ticket to visit."

"He bought you a ticket to visit? When?" I asked.

"I fly tonight, last minute thing. Don't worry, I'm not cramping my big brother's style, I'm staying with Camilla."

"Camilla? Who the fuck is Camilla?"

"A cousin, distant I think, someone on Geraldo's side. Anyway, we need to talk. I'll call you as soon as I arrive."

"What do you mean we need to talk? Is Mamma okay?"

"Yes, just some decisions about the farm. Don't panic, I'll call as soon as I arrive."

We said our goodbyes and I immediately telephoned Geraldo. Something didn't add up. Adriana had never left the village other than the monthly trip to the city. There was no way she would be flying miles just for a visit.

"Rocco, I was expecting your call," Geraldo said after I had announced myself.

"Why is Adriana coming here?" I asked.

"Two reasons: your Mamma feels she is getting too close to a boy, an unsuitable boy, and she wants to talk about selling off part of the farm. It's too much for her. I'm advising, of course, but she wants your thoughts."

"Okay, I think she should sell the farm. And as for Adriana, I want to know what boy."

"The boy will be dealt with, don't worry about that. Now, how is life in America?"

We chatted back and forth. He kept in contact with Joe so was well aware of how life in America was but it was nice to talk to him. We spoke about once a month normally but it was the first I'd heard about selling off part of the farm. I sighed, perhaps I should return, just for a visit to help. I trusted Geraldo of course but I hadn't spoken to Mamma for a while.

****

The following day a taxi deposited Adriana at the doorstep to the office. I was annoyed; I would have collected her. She was too headstrong and I was unhappy that she had made the trip alone.

"Rocco," she said as she flung herself into my arms. She then started to cry.

"What's up, why are you crying?" I asked, concerned.

"I'm in love, Rocco, and Mamma hates him. Everyone hates him but he loves me and I want to be with him."

I sighed, so she had come all this way because she was in love and no one liked him.

"Tell me about him."

Between her sobs she told me about an English man she had met, he was holidaying in Italy, backpacking his way around, and she had fallen in love with him. He was earning money by working in bars and restaurants. She wanted to marry him, not that he had asked her of course.

"How can you marry a man when he hasn't asked?" I said.

"He loves me, I know he does."

"Have you slept with him?"

"Rocco, what a question to ask. I don't ask about your personal life, do I?"

She was cross but I guessed the answer was that she had. Mamma must have found out and was probably distraught. No wonder she had been sent away. But America? I guessed Mamma had no idea of the trouble Adriana could get in to if she put her mind to it.

The office door opened, Adriana took a slight step away from me as I turned to look.

"I, erm, I'm sorry. I'll come back later," Evelyn said.

She backed out of the office as quickly as she could. It wasn't hard to miss the shock on her face though.

"Who's that?" Adriana asked.

"Joe's daughter. Wait here, I need to see what she wanted."

I followed Evelyn and watched as she ducked down an alley. She leant against the wall and angrily brushed tears from her eyes.

"Bastard," she whispered.

"Who? Me?" I asked. I had startled her.

"She's my sister, Evelyn. You ran before I could introduce you," I added.

"Oh, I..." She didn't finish her sentence before I closed the gap between us.

My hand snaked around her neck; my fingers pushed her chin up so she would look me in the eyes. I was powerless, I needed to kiss her. My lips gently brushed against hers as her hand grabbed the hair at the nape of my neck and pulled my head closer to hers. Before our kiss deepened I heard laughter. I raised my face. Evelyn was better than a kiss in a dirty alley.

"What did you want to see me for?" I asked.

Her arms fell to her side and she sighed. I took a step back, placing a respectable distance between us.

"I wanted to see a movie tonight. I need a car."

Evelyn had never been to the movies on her own and she had no need to ask my permission to use a car. I was aware—no, *hoped*—her request was just an excuse to see me.

"Who are you going with?" I was responsible for her safety, it was important that I knew—or perhaps I wanted to be sure it wasn't another man.

"No one. I just want to do something this evening."

"You can't go to the movies alone, Evelyn."

"I can. I don't exactly have a list of friends to invite, do I?"

There was bitterness to her voice and I felt sorry for her. She didn't have a list of friends; I was aware how isolated she had become. Partly because she had taken over her mother's role and partly because our life meant friends were not welcome.

"How about dinner?" I asked.

"Dinner?"

"Yes, you know that thing we do in the evenings. I'll pick you up at seven," I said with a chuckle.

"Okay, that would be lovely," she replied.

I gave her a brief kiss to her cheek; I wouldn't cheapen her any further by mauling her in an alley like a whore. If I was to do what I wanted, to have a relationship with her, it needed to be done right.

****

Adriana had planned an evening with the distant cousin, someone I was yet to meet. I took myself back to the house I was staying in. I had a couple of hours before I was to meet Evelyn and as I lay on the bed after my shower I started to panic. I ran through various lines in my head, excuses should anyone report back to Joe that they had seen me with her.

I was just entertaining her as a friend, as the daughter of the man that held my safety in his hands.

I decided it was safer to drive my self, there would be less explaining to do, so grabbed the keys to the Mercedes before leaving the house. It surprised me to feel nervous; my palms sweated a little as I made my way to the house.

Although Paulo was stationed at the house, he was under my command; he wouldn't talk unless I told him to. I let myself in the front door and walked to the kitchen following the subtle scent of her perfume. Evelyn was sat at the table; she wore a white dress with big red flowers on it. The colour set off her olive skin—she looked stunning, like a fifties pin-up.

"You look beautiful, Evelyn," I said.

"Thank you," she replied before lowering her head to conceal the blush.

I chuckled. "Come on, we don't want to be late."

I placed my hand on her lower back as I guided her to the car, opening the passenger door and helping her in. Nerves started to get to me and in one way it agitated me. Why was I nervous? I fiddled with a packet trying to shake loose a cigarette.

"Do you mind?" I said, forgetting for a moment that she might.

"No, of course not. Where are we going?" she asked.

"A little place I know. Quiet, but you'll like it. They have the best veal."

We settled in a comfortable silence as we made our way to Great Falls. Fredrico's was just the place I needed. It was secluded, out of the way and I knew we would have the privacy I desired.

We were ushered to a table at the back of the restaurant; bread and a small bowl of oil were placed on the table. I tore off a piece of bread, dipped it in the oil before offering it to her.

"Here, taste," I said. I let my fingers linger on her soft lips.

"The oil is from my family farm," I told her.

Joe had decided that was a way to help support my family. He purchased all the oil they could make, giving my mother a decent income.

"Tell me about them?" Evelyn asked.

Perhaps the anguish on my face as I thought of my family was obvious. "You don't have to," she added.

I tried hard not to let my emotions show as I recalled that night and what followed.

"My father was murdered, Evelyn. My brother too. They came early one evening, dragged them from the house in front of my mother, my sister and me. I watched as they were taken away. I never saw them alive again. I'll never forget my mother's screams as she tried to wrestle with them, before they threw her to the ground."

It was difficult; the years had not diminished the anger I felt. For a long time I had wanted to bury my brother next to his father, to give him a resting place and somewhere for my mother to mourn him. For me, that was the ultimate insult. They had returned my father but not his son.

Evelyn held my hand in hers. The whole time I had spoken she'd ran her thumb over my knuckles. I stared at her hand, so delicate in mine.

"I waited years and then I got my revenge."

"And then you came here," she said.

"Yes, your father knew my uncle. My mother sent me here to protect me, to make sure I was safe."

"I'm glad she did."

Menus were placed on the table and our conversation returned to normal topics. She was easy to chat to, we laughed and ate—it was nice to be able to enjoy a normal evening with her until the conversation turned to her father.

"Speaking of your father, I don't think he would be pleased to know you were here with me," I said.

She sighed and I was aware of the shift in atmosphere; we finished our coffee in silence. When it was time to leave I took some bills from my wallet, left them on the table and held out my hand. We walked from the restaurant but instead of heading to the car I led her to a small park area and sat on the bench.

"Thank you for tonight. I've really enjoyed myself," she said.

"It was a pleasure, Evelyn. It's nice to be able to relax and enjoy myself."

My arm was slung over the back of the bench and my fingers ran across the top of her shoulder. I turned towards her. Her eyes, so full of trust, fixed on mine. Her lips parted slightly as I leant towards her. She placed her hand on my cheek and I leant into it. I wanted her—I wanted to love her.

Our kiss was deep and her hands gripped the front of my shirt, pulling me towards her. She would have given herself to me there and then and it was that thought running through my mind that made me stop. I pulled away.

"I need to get you home, Evelyn, it's getting late," I whispered.

"I don't have a curfew," she protested.

"No, but if we stay here any longer I'm going to do something we both might regret."

As soon as the words left my lips, I regretted them. It wasn't what I meant. I had no time to explain and no words to convey how I felt, how conflicted I was. She stood and walked back towards the car. I sat for a moment with my eyes closed. The situation was dangerous—she was dangerous. She was like a drug to me and I wanted her. I hated that I wanted her, because I knew—deep down I could never have her. We drove the short way home in silence.

Before the car had pulled to a stop, she reached for the door handle. I placed my hand on her thigh. I needed to explain.

"Wait, you misunderstand me."

"What do I misunderstand, Rocco? You kiss me like you mean it. You tell me 'soon' and leave me for days on end. You play me like I have no feelings."

Her voice had risen in anger and I wanted her even more then. My cock strained against the zipper of my trousers, my heart pounded in my chest as I looked at her face, her eyes no longer trusting but full of spirit.

"Oh I mean it, Evelyn. Every second your mouth is mine don't you think I want more? Don't you think I want to throw you down and take you there and then? I want your body; I want every inch of you. I want to taste you, to fuck you. I want to own you. I want to be your first."

"Then why don't you?" she whispered.

"Because your father would kill me."

There was a moment of silence; we were both desperately trying to control ourselves. I meant every word I'd said. Right at that moment I wanted to rip that pretty dress from her body, I wanted to fuck her, to make her mine. I wanted to take her virginity and shout from the fucking rooftops that it was mine—she was mine. If only the risk was my life, I would have done it. My mother's face flashed through my mind. If Joe sent me home, she would be burying another son. I sat back in my seat.

She pushed the car door open so violently it sprung back and caught her shin; her cry of pain tore through me. I opened my door and ran around the car, by that point she had limped to the front door of her house. She fumbled with the key, not quite getting it into the lock so I leant over her shoulder, took the key from her and opened the door. Without a word she walked in, closing the door behind her.

I stood looking at the closed door. As much as I would be eternally grateful to Joe for taking me in, I would never be able to have the one thing I desired. I walked back to the car, wound down the window and lit a cigarette before driving home.

"Fuck," I shouted as I exited the car, slamming the door so hard the window rattled.

I was angry with myself and angry at the situation I had found myself in. I opened the front door and headed straight to the bedroom. I fell on the bed fully clothed and thoughts whirled through my mind. I could smell her and I could taste her on my lips. Her scent was driving me mad. I didn't get any sleep that night.

****

The following morning I sat with a coffee in the courtyard out back and watched the sun rise. I had thought, pondered and argued with myself the whole night. I'd made a decision. Leaving my coffee cup on the small metal bistro table, I grabbed my car keys and left the house. I needed to see her. I had to take the risk.

As I approached Joe's I saw Evelyn on the other side of the road. She was dressed conservatively, and despite the sunny day, wore a cardigan. I had to drive a little way before being able to make a U-turn and it was then that I saw her walk up the steps of the church. I sat in the car wrestling with my decision.

When I could wrestle no more, I walked to the church door, quietly entered and stood at the back watching her. Her head was bowed; her hands were clasped in her lap as she sat in a pew just a few feet away from me. Before the service had finished she stood to leave, heading my way. She was alongside me before realising I was there. I reached out and pulled her into the alcove I'd been hiding.

"Here for forgiveness?" she spat, that feisty spirit showed in her face.

"Yes."

"For what we've done?" There was a hurt tone to her voice.

"No, for what I'm about to do."

I took her hand and led her to the car. Opening the passenger door, I guided her in. Neither of us spoke as we made our way back to my house.

Before the front door had closed behind us, I took her hands and backed her to the hall wall. Our kiss was feverish, she moaned and the sound reverberated through me. There was no going back as I led her to the bedroom.

"Is your sister here?" she asked.

"She's staying with a cousin."

I took a deep breath. As much as it was clear she wanted me, I had to take it slow. I unbuttoned her cardigan, sliding it from her shoulders before reaching around and finding the zip of her dress. The dress pooled around her feet and she crossed her arms over her chest. I peeled them away, holding them to her sides. I wanted to look at her, to admire every inch of her body. I smiled as the blush crept up her chest.

After pulling my t-shirt over my head, I took her hands and placed them on my chest; for some strange reason it seemed important that she touched me, that she felt my heartbeat under her fingertips. She traced the tattoos and I held my breath as her hands lowered to the top of my jeans. She undid the zip and they fell to the floor, my cock sprung free. Her eyes widened as her hand reached down and closed around it.

"You can stop this anytime you want. Just say the word, Evelyn," I whispered.

She swallowed hard, licked her lips before reaching behind and unclipping her bra with shaking hands. She kept eye contact as she hooked her fingers on either side of her panties and slid them down her legs. Her body shook with nerves or excitement, I couldn't tell, as she stood before me naked. She was beautiful, stunning, and curvy—a hundred words ran through my mind, none of which could describe how perfect she was.

Closing in on her, she had no choice but to back up until her legs hit the side of the bed. I held one arm around her waist as she gently fell. With a nervous giggle she shuffled on to the bed until she was lying on her back looking up at me.

I crawled up her body, taking hold of her arms and raising them above her head. My lips trailed a path down her neck, across her collarbone and slowly down her chest. I sucked on a hard nipple and heard her gasp with pleasure. She raised her body forcing her nipple further into my mouth. I needed to taste her though.

I moved down her body leaving small kisses across her stomach, dipped my tongue in her navel before moving to the top of her thigh. She tensed, her hands gripped the bedding and I saw her screw her eyes shut.

"Relax," I whispered.

I inhaled her scent, an intoxicating scent. She was wet as I parted her and ran my nose over her clitoris. My tongue licked and she cried out. As her body arched off the bed, I ran my thumb over her clitoris and my tongue probed deeper inside her. I couldn't get enough of her, of her taste, of her smell, of the most intimate place on her body.

When her cries turned into a sob, I moved back up to her face and kissed her. Her arms gripped around my body and her nails dug into my back as the tip of my cock brushed against her.

"Are you sure?" I asked. She nodded.

I reached over to the bedside cabinet drawer and pulled out a condom; I tore it open and rolled it down my cock. Holding her hands above her head again I gently pushed into her, slowly at first. She tensed, she sucked in a breath and bit down on her lip not quite able to stifle the yelp as I gave one thrust then stilled.

"Okay?" I whispered. Again, she nodded her head.

As she began to relax, she matched my thrusts, raising her hips to meet mine. She was so hot, so tight and so wet. There was no way I was going to last, especially when she wrapped her legs around mine, opening herself further to me. My stomach tightened and my cock pulsed as I came—I called out her name as my body shuddered.

I collapsed on top of her and smiled at the most wonderful sound. She was laughing.

"This is going to sting," I said as I pulled out.

I watched her wince as I rolled to my side, depositing the condom on the floor next to the bed. I wrapped her in my arms.

"How do you feel?" I asked.

"Wonderful, sore," she replied with a laugh.

I chuckled as she rested her head on my shoulder and placed her arm across my chest. I listened as her breathing deepened and she drifted off into sleep.

****

I watched her sleep. Her long dark eyelashes shimmered, wet from tears that gently rolled down her cheeks. I caught one on my thumb and raised it to my lips. My grandmother used to say, "Tears are from the soul." I wanted part of Evelyn's soul—it was pure and kind. Her eyes fluttered open.

"Hey, don't cry. It wasn't that bad was it?" I asked.

"No, I don't know why I'm crying," she laughed as she spoke.

"Come on, let me run you a bath. It'll help."

She sat on the edge of the bed and I watched her cheeks colour a bright red. She'd held her hand in her lap and her eyes were wide with alarm. Her fingertips were as red as her cheeks with blood.

"It's okay, that's normal," I said.

I held out my hand. She was reluctant at first to move. I laughed to ease her embarrassment and led her to the bathroom.

"I need to pee," she said.

"So, pee," I replied as I poured bubble bath under the running water.

Evelyn hopped from foot to foot.

"Evelyn, I've just had my tongue inside you, you came in my mouth. It's a bit late to be embarrassed to pee in front of me," I said.

She covered her face as she giggled and it was such a wonderful sound. She climbed in the bath and sat between my legs resting back on my chest. As I wrapped my arms around her a thought flashed through my mind—we fitted together. Every part of her body melded into mine, she was my perfect fit.

"I'm sorry, I didn't do…you know…anything to you," she whispered.

I felt her cringe as she spoke.

"You did the ultimate, Evelyn. You gave your virginity to me."

We fell silent for a while.

I slid one hand down her stomach and the other caressed her breast. Her body responded immediately to my touch. Her nipple hardened and she moaned as my fingers gently squeezed her clitoris.

"You are so responsive," I whispered into her neck.

Evelyn moved her hand to cover mine—our fingers were entwined.

"You do it," I said. I knew she had done this to herself before, I'd watched that one time in the shower.

My cock was rigid in my hand as I watched her bring herself to another orgasm. The sound of her moans and the laughter that followed would stay with me forever. Whether it was her moans of pleasure or the laughter that brought me to my release I wasn't sure, but it felt so good. I laughed with her.

When the water cooled I climbed out. There wasn't the soft fluffy towels that she was used to in my bathroom, instead old scratchy ones was all I had. I wrapped one around her. As we walked back to the bedroom I heard her stomach grumble.

"You dress. I'm going to prepare lunch," I said.

I threw on a pair of jeans and leaving her to dress, headed downstairs. Evelyn joined me in the courtyard just a few minutes later. I had laid out plates of meat, olives and breads. I poured us both a glass of wine and we sat soaking up the afternoon sun.

"Tell me about your village," she asked.

"You would love it, Evelyn. We're on top of a mountain, a river of pure, ice-cold water flows through the middle. Everyone owns a farm, not large but enough to grow grapes or olives, fruit and vegetables. Of course everyone knows everyone and their business," I said with a laugh.

"It sounds idyllic."

"It was. I miss it sometimes. I miss the smell of the lemon trees in the evening, the sound of insects outside my bedroom window at night. I even miss the heat of summer. It get's so hot that it's hard to breathe."

I was aware I was rambling and it was when I saw a look of sadness cross her face that I realised perhaps I shouldn't have said how much I miss the village. The sound of a ringing telephone interrupted us.

I placed my hand on her cheek, ran my thumb over her lips to brush away a crumb before rising and making my way to the hall and picking up the telephone.

"Rocco, I need advice," I heard.

Sammy was the newest member of our family. A young, hot headed Italian from the neighbourhood. Whereas Joe, the guys and me preferred a subtle existence, Sammy loved nothing more than to shoot his mouth off about who he worked for. He wouldn't last too long in the family.

"What do you need?"

"There's a girl. Fuck, Rocco, she's bleeding real bad. I don't know what to do."

"What do you mean there's a girl. What the fuck have you done?"

"She wanted it rough, know what I mean? Now she's bleeding."

"Where are you?"

"I'm at the hotel. Shall I call the manager?"

"For fuck's sake, Sammy, I'm busy. Can't you deal with it? You're a fucking liability. I'll be there in half an hour. Try not to fuck up in that time."

The guy was a dumb as shit—*call the manager?* I slammed the phone back into its cradle. I had to stand in the cool hallway for a moment to calm myself down. If what I suspected had happened, and it would be the second time, Sammy needed to disappear. I made a call; I informed Jonathan of the situation and Mack to meet me.

"I have to go. Business," I said to Evelyn as I joined her in the kitchen. She had washed the dishes.

I drove with one hand, the other holding Evelyn's. Our fingers were laced together. Once we had pulled to a halt outside her house, I lifted her chin, tilted her face towards mine. Our kiss was all too brief.

"I'll see you tomorrow. What time do you finish work?" I asked.

"Five, normally."

"Okay, I'll see you at five then. I'll pick you up."

I watched her walk to the door. Joey came running down the path and jumped into her arms as I drove away; her laughter followed me.

"So, what's up?" Mack asked as I pulled onto his drive and he opened the car door.

"Sammy's fucked up again. I got a call about some girl and she's bleeding. That's all I know right now."

"Shit. Where?"

"The hotel of all places. Get in." Mack climbed into the passenger seat.

Joe owned a hotel in the city. It was popular with tourists and having a bleeding girl in one of the rooms was not going to be good for business. I left the car outside the hotel entrance and we made our way to reception. I couldn't fail to notice the lick of the lips, the tucking of hair behind the ear from the receptionist. I wasn't interested in her; she had tried on many occasions to get my attention.

"Suite key," I demanded. It was with a scowl that she handed it over.

"He booked himself into the suite?" Mack asked.

"Normally does. I'm going to make sure it comes out of his earnings."

The elevator opened opposite the suite door, which was opened before we had even got to it. Sammy stood there in just shorts; blood was spattered over his chest. I pushed past him. There was a naked blonde lying across the bed; her hair covered her face. Purple bruises marked her body and her thighs were smeared with blood.

"What the fuck?" Mack said as he joined me.

I brushed some hair away from her face. She startled and scooted up the bed. The pace that she moved had me back off immediately. I held my hands up in front of me.

"It's okay, I'm here to help you," I gently said.

She sobbed and drew her knees to her chest, dragging the sheet around her body. Her lip was split, one eye half closed and the tears that ran down her face left a clean line in the blood on her cheeks.

As Sammy stepped behind me, I spun around and punched the fucker in the face. He stumbled backwards and I punched again, taking great satisfaction in hearing his nose break, in hearing the crunch of his cheekbone as it shattered under my fist. Finally he fell to my feet and I kicked him as hard as I could in the balls.

"You fucking prick," I said as I spat on him. "We need to take care of her, and get rid of him," I said to Mack.

The girl was shaking, her mouth was open as if trying to scream but no sound came out.

"Let me help you, okay? What's your name?" I spoke quietly trying to calm her.

It took a moment before she could reply.

"Nina," she whispered.

"Nina, can you stand up? Take a shower, clean yourself up a bit."

She nodded but didn't move.

"I'll be in the other room. My name is Rocco. Don't you worry about that prick in there, he can't hurt you now. You call me when you're done, okay?"

I left the room closing the door behind me. Sammy was sat on the sofa, his head in his hands as blood dripped from his nose to the cream carpet.

"Is she okay?" he asked, his voice strained by his injuries.

"Don't fucking speak. Don't open your mouth in my presence, you hear me?" I said as I slapped the side of his head.

I paced the living room trying to control the anger that raged inside me. I hated any abuse of women, as did Joe. He would be fucking livid to know what went on in his hotel.

"Is she a whore?" I asked.

Sammy stayed quiet. "Answer me, you prick."

"You told me not to speak."

I punched him to the side of his head and he fell sideways on the couch.

"Don't play fucking smart with me."

"Yeah, so why all the fuss?" he said, wincing as he spoke.

"Why all the fuss? She's a fucking woman, doesn't matter what she does for a job. She's someone's daughter, sister." I shouted at him.

I was about to kick the shit out of him when the bedroom door opened slightly. I walked towards it. Nina had dressed and her hair, still wet from her shower, was pulled back in a ponytail. Without make-up she looked so young. I walked into the bedroom; she backed away with every step I took.

"How old are you?" I asked.

"Nineteen," she answered.

"Why, why do you do this?"

"Do what? Did you think I asked to be beaten?" Her voice rose in anger.

"No, you know what I mean. Why do you sell yourself?"

"I'm in college and I have a kid without a father, why do you think?"

I stood and walked to the bedside table. Picking up Sammy's wallet I counted out all the notes he had. I placed over five hundred dollars on the bed.

"He owes you that."

"I don't want his money. I just want to go home."

"You might not want his money but I bet your kid could do with new shoes, your college fees can get paid. Take it."

She scooped the money into her purse and hesitated before a mirror on the wall. I saw the tears brimming in her eyes as she touched her face.

"I can't walk through this hotel," she said, her voice cracked.

"I'll walk with you, drive you home."

She looked at my reflection in the mirror for a while before nodding.

"Mack, maybe Sammy might like to visit Fredrico," I said as I walked through the living room. Mack smiled.

"I'll take Nina home and get Paulo to meet you here. Give that prick some time to clean himself up a little," I added.

Nina and I took the stairs all the way to the basement avoiding reception. I pushed open a fire exit that took us back on the sidewalk. Opening the car door, I waited for her to climb in. She hesitated.

"I can walk from here," she said.

"You could barely walk from the room. I'm not going to hurt you."

"I saw the way you beat him," the tone of her voice displayed her fear.

"He deserved that. I beat him for what he did to you. If you want to walk, fine, but I'm offering you a lift home if you want it."

She looked at me for a moment longer before climbing in the car.

We drove in silence other than Nina giving directions until we pulled up at an apartment block. I knew the area in Columbia Heights; she was a tenant of Joe's. Maybe that's how she'd got involved with Sammy, he collected rent.

"You're a good man, Rocco. Thank you," Nina said as she exited the car.

I shrugged my shoulders and watched as she entered the apartment door. Turning the car around I headed for Jonathan's. Sammy would need to be replaced.

Chapter Five

The following morning I sat in the office. Ricardo, or Richard as he preferred to be called, was instructed to take over the rentals. Before he left, I handed him a note; he was to give it to Nina. I had paid for a year's rental on her apartment. There were a thousand women out there in the same situation, kids, no money, school and no jobs who had to sell themselves. I couldn't help them all; I didn't want to help them all. Some loved the lifestyle they led but there was something about Nina that had me wanting to help. She was doing something not by choice but by necessity.

As the office emptied I turned to Jonathan. "I have a problem."

"Go on," he replied.

"Evelyn."

"Ah, yes. I've seen the looks. You know she's only eighteen, don't you?"

"I know but…"

"Don't go there, Rocco. Not unless you are in love with her and plan on marrying the girl. You break her and Joe will break you."

I sighed. Was I in love with her? I was certainly infatuated with her, in lust with her, but I'd never been in love. I had no idea what that was meant to feel like.

"Rocco, she's not the type of girl you can have a fling with."

"I know that. What if I was in love with her, what would Joe say?"

"I can't answer that. He might have been in the US for some time but he's an old fashioned Italian at heart. He wants her to marry, I know that much."

"He has hopes of her marrying a doctor or a lawyer. I mean, how realistic is that?"

"It's not, I think he just hopes for something different for her. Look, we know that's not going to happen. A lawyer? Fuck me, Rocco, unless he was in the family, we'd all end up in prison," Jonathan laughed.

****

The day wore on, paperwork was done, orders placed and rents collected. I checked my watch noticing it was nearing five o'clock.

"I need to go," I said.

Jonathan looked up from a stack of receipts. "Be careful, Rocco."

I nodded and headed to my car. It was a short journey to Richmond Inc., the company Joe owned, the company Evelyn worked at. I parked outside and exactly at five walked through the door. Evelyn was sat at reception, Mark on the edge of her desk. I didn't like his proximity to her. He sprung to his feet.

"Rocco, I wasn't expecting you," he said.

"I'm not here for you," I replied.

Evelyn looked from him to me; the tension in the air was obvious. She coughed, clearing her throat before gathering her bag and rounding the desk. She bade a goodnight and we left.

"What was that all about?" she asked.

"Nothing. Business," I replied.

I took her hand and led her to the car not giving a fuck if Philips was watching. She was mine; I wanted him to know that.

"Did you have a good day?" I asked as we pulled into the traffic.

"The usual. I love working there but Mr. Philips is so disorganised."

I wanted to disagree. Mark wasn't disorganised by nature, more on purpose. Things didn't add up in that warehouse and I was beginning to get suspicious. Goods were making their way out the back door and not being accounted for. We pulled up outside the address Adriana had given me.

"I have to collect my sister; she needs to return to Italy tomorrow. I thought she could come to dinner with us. You can get to know each other."

I hadn't intentionally decided that Adriana was to meet Evelyn, she had a big mouth. I had no doubt the village would know the minute she returned. I wanted to see her on her last night and I wanted to see Evelyn. I was taking a gamble on combing the two.

Adriana came bounded down the front steps as I climbed from the car.

"I have a friend with me, Joe's daughter, Evelyn. She's coming with us," I said.

"A friend?" Adriana said with a laugh.

"Yes, she's just a friend."

Adriana climbed into the back of the car. "Evelyn, I'm Adriana. It's good to meet you."

"It's good to meet you too," Evelyn replied.

I pulled away from the drive when Adriana started to speak in our own dialect. Evelyn may be Italian, and I knew could speak the language, but she wouldn't understand our dialect.

"English or Italian, Adriana," I said.

"I'm sorry, Evelyn, sometimes I forget. Rocco, Mamma has been on the phone. She wants you to call."

"I will, later."

I drove to a pizzeria with a courtyard in the back. It was a nice autumn day and the sun was still high. Adriana rambled on about village life. There was no more mention of the Englishman, instead she was now into American TV and could I persuade Mamma to invest in one.

"You won't get the same programmes back home," I reminded her.

I loved my sister but when she was in company she was excitable, she chatted non-stop. She included Evelyn in the conversation though, which pleased me. With our meal finished, I stood to leave.

"Oh, not time to go home already? Can we go to a bar?" Adriana said.

"No, you're too young for bars," I replied.

"You must bring Evelyn home, Rocco, meet Mamma."

I glared at her. "Come on, it's time to go."

Her comment had annoyed me. I had told her Evelyn was just a friend and she wouldn't know if Evelyn knew my reason for leaving the village. There was no way I was ever going to risk taking her to my village and Adriana would know that. Despite chatting all the way back to where she had been staying, Adriana knew she had riled me. She could be very manipulative when she wanted to be.

"I'll collect you later, drive you to the airport," I said as we pulled on the drive.

Adriana lent forwards and kissed my cheek, she did the same to Evelyn then, after giving me a wink, she left the car. I guessed I was brooding and before I knew it, in silence, we had arrived back at my house.

"Sorry, I don't like that she's going home. I wanted her and my mother to come here, to leave the farm, but Mamma won't," I said by way of an explanation.

"Will your uncle look after them?" she asked.

"Yes, but I know they would be safer here. Come on, I don't want to talk about them anymore, it'll spoil the evening."

We made our way into the house and once the front door was closed, I pulled her into my arms. She calmed me; she stilled the anger and sadness that had flooded my body earlier.

"What do you want to do?" I asked.

It was the smirk on her lips, the glint in her eye that had me laughing. She raised her eyebrows at me—she wanted me and that was a feeling that I liked, a lot.

Taking her hand, I led her to the bedroom. She bunched my t-shirt in her hands, raising it over my head; she kissed me as I undid the buttons of her blouse. I unclipped her bra, the need to feel her bare skin under my hand was consuming me. I cupped a breast, her soft skin too tempting. I lowered my head, taking a hard nipple in my mouth as she popped the buttons on her trousers.

She gripped my hair pulling my head to hers. Her kiss was feverish, that time she took control and walked me backwards to the bed until I fell. I watched her strip for me; she took her time, each movement slow and deliberate until she was naked. I reached forward grabbing her wrist and pulling her on top of me. It was when she ground herself against me that I moaned.

Rising onto her knees she ran her hands down my chest, over my stomach to the top of my jeans. Way too slowly she unbuttoned them, teasing me. I raised my hips to allow her to pull them down. She ran her fingertips around the waistband of my shorts sliding them down my legs. I kicked them off; they joined my jeans at the bottom of the bed.

She lowered her head and her long hair brushed against my skin like a feather. She kissed my stomach; her soft lips had my skin electrified. Her mouth moved down to my cock. Her tongue played over the tip, lapping up a small bead of fluid before she opened her mouth and lowered her head.

I winced as her teeth ran along the underside of my cock, a little too rough.

"Gently," I said.

She flattened her tongue using it as a shield as she sucked my cock. Her hot mouth tightened around me. I gripped her hair, raised my hips and she took me further into her mouth.

I needed to come, I pulled her head away and she replaced her mouth with her hand. She gently grasped and stroked, I covered her hand with mine and guided her. She cupped my balls with her other, her nails gently scraping over the skin. I couldn't hold back any longer and I called out her name as I came. I couldn't supress the laughter as I watched her. She was fascinated by the milky fluid that ran through her fingers, her thumb spread my come across her palm. I handed her some tissues.

"Your turn," I said.

Evelyn lay beside me, I propped myself on one elbow as my hand trailed down her stomach to her already parted legs. She was so wet; her juices had smeared on her thighs. I resisted the urge to lick her clean; instead I fucked her with my fingers. To feel her, to watch her arch her body from the bed and call out my name washed anyway any doubt I had. To see her give herself to me freely, surrendering herself, caused my heart to ache.

It was when she cried, when she fell apart around my fingers, when she came and called out my name, that I knew I loved her.

Before she could compose herself I moved on top of her. I rolled a condom down my cock as quick as possible and pushed into her. I needed to fuck her, to own her, to posses her. She met my thrusts; she wrapped her legs around my waist encouraging me deeper, faster and harder. Her nails scraped down my back, the sting spurred me on until sweat rolled from my forehead. She came, I came. At that moment, my heart broke.

My heart broke not because I couldn't love her the way she needed, not because I wouldn't marry her, but because I didn't believe we had a future.

****

I didn't see Evelyn the following day and I ached for her. I ached for her touch, her smell and just to hear her voice. Joe was returning from his meeting. I was to meet him and bring him up to speed on business. I had hoped that meeting would have been at the office. I was dismayed to find out he wanted to return home, to meet there. I wasn't avoiding Evelyn; I was avoiding her father noticing any attraction between us.

Joe opened the front door and was immediately assaulted by Joey. Evelyn followed behind and into her father's embrace. She smiled over to me; I ignored her for fear of giving anything away. I saw her frown and it pained me. She took Joey from Joe and headed to the kitchen, we entered Joe's office.

"So, Rocco, I hear you have a girlfriend," he said.

I said the first thing that came to mind. "No, just having a bit of fun, Joe. No one important."

I hadn't finished my sentence when Evelyn came in the office with a tray of coffee. She gasped and I watched her hands shake, the coffee spill and burn her fingers.

"Always so clumsy," Joe said with a shake of his head.

She rushed from the room; I wanted to follow her, to check she was okay and to explain. I sat for five maybe ten minutes before the urge to see her took over.

"Need a piss," I said as I stood.

I closed the office door behind me and headed for the kitchen. Evelyn was nowhere to be seen. I crept upstairs, her bedroom door was ajar but she wasn't there.

"She's gone," I heard.

Maria had opened her bedroom door so silently, I hadn't realised she was watching me.

"Gone where?"

"I don't know, she's gone out. I saw her leave," she replied before closing her door again.

I made my way back to the office, concerned. Evelyn was an adult, she was entitled to leave her own home whenever she wanted but she had heard what I'd said and I wanted to explain my reasons for saying it.

Our meeting went on, it grew dark and with that my anxiety increased. Evelyn should have been home. Joe called for her as he wanted more coffee, but received no answer. He searched the house as I had done to be told by Maria that she had left hours ago.

"Evelyn is out alone in the dark," he said as he returned to the office.

"I'll go and see if I can find her. She probably got caught up with a friend," I said.

I noticed Jonathan look at me but avoided his stare. I pulled on a jacket and lit a cigarette as I walked to my car. The night was chilly and I hoped she had thought to take a coat with her. I was annoyed, angry that she had run off, but most of that anger was because I worried for her. As safe as DC was during the day, as safe as the family made the streets, there was always someone wanting either revenge or to make a point and whether she realised or not, Evelyn was an easy target. She had more freedom than most in her position.

I drove up and down the streets, searched in the most obvious places I could think of. I checked a couple of bars knowing she wouldn't be there alone but ticking them off my list. I cruised past the church, it's doors long since locked but it was place she found calming. Eventually I decided to head back to the house in case I had missed her. Jonathan met me on the drive.

"She's back, came home half an hour ago," he said.

"Thank fuck for that."

"I don't know what's going on, Rocco, but you need to be careful."

"Jonathan, I love her but I know we can't be together. I'll stay away for a few days. I need to think, maybe I need to end this."

"Have you…" Jonathan didn't need to finish his sentence. I nodded.

He sighed. "You'll break her heart," he said.

"I know, but what choice do I have?"

"Talk to Joe?"

"She's eighteen, he would never give his blessing."

With that I left and a sadness engulfed me. I'd said aloud what I felt and that love wouldn't fade overnight, if it ever did.

Chapter Six

It seemed that I was being kept away from the house and I wondered if Jonathan had told Joe. I kept myself busy but no matter what I did I couldn't erase Evelyn from my mind. She occupied my thoughts night and day. The evenings were worse, I could smell her in my bed, on the pillow that I hugged to me each night afraid to wash it and lose her. I lasted four days.

I'd been at the club; initially to check on stock but a few whiskeys later I had an idea. It was early hours of the morning when I drove to Joe's. I had the window wound down allowing the night air to fill the car and sober me up. I was being reckless I knew that, but the desire to see her out-weighed getting caught.

The house was in darkness; there was no sign of anyone still awake as I quietly entered. I crept up the stairs remembering which one creaked and avoiding it. I paused outside her bedroom door. It was at the opposite end of the house to Joe's and I thanked my lucky stars for that. I opened the door as quietly as I could and closed it behind me. I stood for a moment allowing my eyes to adjust. The drapes were open and the moon shone through illuminating her. She had thrown the sheets from the bed and wore a thin t-shirt, a t-shirt that once belonged to me.

Her hair fanned out over the white pillowslips, one arm was thrown over her head as she lay on her back. The t-shirt did nothing to conceal the white cotton panties she wore.

I moved to the side of the bed. At first I just wanted to look at her but as I kneeled, she stirred.

I placed my hand over her mouth as she opened her eyes.

"Shush, it's just me," I said as I removed my hand. I hadn't wanted her to scream out in fright.

"What are you doing here?" she whispered.

"I couldn't stay away. I tried but I can't."

I sat on the edge of her bed and ran my hands through my hair. She reached for a bedside lamp.

"You're drunk," she said.

"No, I was but not now. I needed to see you."

"You've ignored me all week. Why now? It's the middle of the night."

"I'm sorry, Evelyn. We need to talk but I think your father knows. He's kept me away from the house. I've tried to find a reason to come here and he seems to be blocking it." It wasn't entirely true but in my sleep-depraved brain it seemed to make sense at the time.

She sat up and as she did the t-shirt rose, bunching around her waist, exposing the smooth skin of her thigh. I placed my hand on it, my thumb just brushed against the cotton of her panties.

"No, if you want to talk, that's what we'll do," she said as she pushed my hand away.

"Not here, Ev. If he catches me in your bedroom, that will be it for us."

"Tomorrow then. Find an excuse to pick me up from work. I'll tell Papa that I'm going straight out, I won't be home for dinner."

I rested my hand on the side of her face, leant forward and kissed her gently.

"Tomorrow," I whispered.

****

I was on edge the whole day at the office, checking my watch frequently. Twice Joe had spoken to me and I hadn't heard. It was Jonathan kicking me under the desk that brought me back to attention.

"Rocco, what's on your mind?" Joe asked.

"Nothing, a little tired I guess," I said, giving him a reassuring smile.

"Maybe a woman kept him up late," he said with a laugh to Jonathan.

I tried very hard not to show any emotion. Jonathan glared at me and Paulo sniggered.

"Jonathan, let's go home, let Rocco recover from his excesses," Joe said.

I walked with them to the door, the door that Paulo was sitting beside. Closing it behind them I leant down.

"Snigger like that again and I'll cut your fucking throat, understand?" I snarled.

Paulo had seen me with Evelyn; he was not someone I trusted fully.

"Okay, okay," he replied, raising his hands in defence.

I snatched the car keys from the desk and headed out. My car was parked right outside the office in a no stop zone; we never got a ticket of course. The local cops overlooked our parking arrangements. Paulo followed; he would normally drive but I waved him off. I was heading home.

Stripping off, I climbed under the shower. I stood for a while just letting the hot water flow over me. Thoughts of Evelyn's naked body filled my mind and my cock started to twitch. I placed one hand on the tiled wall in front of me, the other I wrapped around my hard cock feeling the silky skin under my fingers. Slowly at first, I ran my hand up and down, my thumb rubbing over the tip. In my mind I saw Evelyn's hand, her mouth stretched around my cock, and her pussy. My mouth watered as I remembered her taste, her smell and how she felt against my tongue.

I stroked harder, faster, allowing the moan to escape that had been building. I felt my stomach tense, my balls tighten and I came. White milky fluid spurted over my hand, mixing with the water from the shower. But it didn't satisfy my desire for her.

At ten minutes before five o'clock I left the house to collect Evelyn. I saw her standing outside her office; she smiled as she crossed the road to join me. I was still tense; my body ached for her touch. At first I didn't speak, she must have thought me such a jerk but I needed to breathe in her scent, to have her calm me. I reached over and took her hand. Just her touch was enough and I took a deep breath in, exhaling slowly.

"Where are we going?" she asked.

"Somewhere hopefully no one knows us," I said with a chuckle.

Joe had recently acquired a new restaurant. The owner could no longer pay the repayments on his loan so Joe had taken over the property. In one way it was a win win situation. The owner got to stay, his apartment was above the restaurant, without the debt strangling him. Okay, so he lost the business he had spent his life building up but he received all the earnings and had to pay rent; rent that was lower than the years of repayments he would have had to make.

Carlo's Kitchen was an old fashioned Italian bistro. Chequered cloths adorned the pine tables; a candle was stuck into the neck of a wine bottle, it gave a romantic glow or maybe hid the stains from previous diners. Despite the décor, the food was good. I opted for a booth, the furthest away from the door and the most secluded.

"I can't be sure but I think your father knows something. He had me running all over the place this week. Whenever I need to speak to him, he arranges to be at the office, never at home."

Maybe I was being paranoid, maybe I was imagining things, but the thought that Joe knew was eating me up.

"Do you think he would really be upset about us?"

I shrugged my shoulders. "I honestly don't know, Evelyn. I do know that he often talks about you meeting a lawyer or a doctor. I doubt he would think I was good enough for you."

"That's just stupid. It's my choice who I see, and come on, can you imagine if I brought a *lawyer* home, a man of the law?" she laughed, the irony was not lost on me.

"What do you know, Ev? About what your father does?"

"Not everything, of course. I know that what he does do isn't legal. I've seen the bundles of money, I've seen the guns, Rocco. And my mother confirmed it when she said, although she loved Papa, this wasn't a life she wanted for me."

Evelyn might as well have stuck a knife through my chest. I recalled hearing those words many years ago and it hurt then.

"I can't help who I fall in love with," she added.

I didn't speak, I couldn't tell her that I loved her back and I wasn't sure why. The words were there, on the tip of my tongue but as I opened my mouth, I swallowed them back down. She went to speak again; I didn't want to hear her retract her words because I hadn't spoken. I placed my fingers over her lips and shook my head.

"You'll have no teeth left if you keep doing that," she said.

I hadn't realised my jaw was so tense my teeth ground together. I laughed and the tension lifted.

"Jonathan's new girlfriend turned up unannounced at the office," I said.

"Oh God, what happened?"

"Well, it was rush to clear away *things*. She's a feisty one. Patricia is her name. Your father likes her."

The longer we sat the more relaxed I became. Although those words, "*I can't help who I fall in love with,*" whirled around my mind. When the meal was eaten and coffee drank, I took her hand and led her from the restaurant. Instead of heading to the car, I took a turn towards a grassy bank. We sat and I placed my arm around her shoulders pulling her close.

"I don't know what the future is, Ev. I want to be honest with you," I said quietly.

"Please, don't say…"

"Hear me out. I don't even have a visa to be here, did you know that? Your father's influence means I haven't already been picked up and sent packing. And that's what bothers me. If I don't have his support, I'm gone. Do you understand what I'm saying?"

"If you want him to know, Rocco, I'll talk to him. He's never refused me."

"And if you're wrong? I feel like I can't let myself fall in love, Evelyn, because I'm too scared that it will be taken away. But I can't let you go either."

We sat in silence for a while. The warmth of her body took the chill from mine. Her head rested on my shoulder and her warm breath caressed the skin on my neck.

"Take me home, Rocco, to your house," she whispered.

I was fucked, doomed; whatever word I chose could not describe how I felt. I loved her yet I couldn't tell her that. I couldn't allow those feelings to come to the surface and it hurt to supress them. In my head I was going round and round in circles—tell Joe, don't tell Joe. I rested my hand on her thigh, her skirt had risen and I felt her smooth skin under my fingers. I ran my hand higher; she sunk lower in the seat inviting me to touch her. I could smell her arousal and I could see the hardness of her nipples through her flimsy top.

Evelyn reached over and placed her hand on my cock as it strained against the tightness of my jeans. I sucked in a breath and pushed my foot down on the gas pedal.

The car was left, parked haphazardly, as I dragged her to the front door. My mouth found hers as I opened it and we stumbled through. It took seconds to discard our clothes as we climbed the stairs. Just a few seconds more to roll down a condom and then fuck her. Her nails raked down my back, joining the scratches she had already left.

"Harder, deeper," she panted. I pulled out of her.

"Get on your knees," I said.

Kneeling on the bed with her perfect ass facing me, she looked stunning. She was giving herself to me anyway I wanted. I slammed into her so fast I heard her gasp. There was nothing nice about what I wanted; I needed to fuck her hard. I'd needed that for hours. I gripped her hips hard enough to bruise as she forced herself back onto my cock. Neither of us seemed to be able to get enough, to get deeper, to get harder or faster. Sweat rolled from my brow, dripped onto her back that was covered in a sheen of perspiration. Her moans grew louder until she was screaming out my name and she came. Her body shook as she fell to her elbows, her legs quivered, and finally I was able to give into my release. I came so hard my stomach was in a knot. I cried out myself.

She collapsed down on the bed; I fell on top of her. We both struggled to get our breathing under control. Evelyn started to giggle, that turned into a laugh until eventually those laughs became sobs. Big, whacking sobs of hopelessness. I rolled to one side and pulled her into my arms. I whispered into her hair as she cried. Her head was buried in my chest and I was glad. I didn't want her to see the tears that rolled down my cheeks. I didn't want her to see the pain I knew would be showing in my eyes. Eventually, we both drifted off to sleep exhausted by our emotions.

****

"Shit, Rocco, wake up. It's gone midnight," I heard, I opened my eyes with a start.

I checked my watch. "Fuck," I said.

Without attempting to clean ourselves, we rushed from the bedroom, gathering our clothes from the hallway, from the stairs. Evelyn was doing the last of her buttons up on her blouse as we bundled into the car. I drove fast, it took half the time, and thankfully the traffic was light. I stopped a couple of doors down from her home.

"I'll walk you," I said.

"No, Papa might see you. I'll be fine from here,"

As she reached to open the door, I wrapped my hand around her neck, pulling me to her for one final deep kiss. I waited until she walked up the drive before turning the car around and heading for home.

****

Over the next few months Jonathan became a close ally, there had been one or two times he had covered for either Evelyn or me. I felt guilty that we were lying to Joe and even guiltier that Jonathan had been brought into our web of deceit. He had covered for me allowing me the afternoon to meet Evelyn, it was a Friday and Joe liked to ease in to the weekend early.

I was parked alongside the church, our regular meeting place when I saw Evelyn with an overnight bag walking towards me.

"What's this?" I asked, taking it from her.

"I'm staying the night, with you," she replied.

"Okay, how did you manage that?"

"Papa thinks I'm with Carmella, someone I knew from school."

"And what if he checks?"

"He won't. He trusts me."

There was a certain irony in that statement and for a moment I saw a flash of pain cross her face. The strain was starting to tell, her eyes had lost a little of their usual sparkle. Another layer of guilt was added.

We arrived at the house and made our way to the kitchen, side by side we made coffee and there was something natural about the way we moved, about the way we did something so ordinary as making coffee. She belonged in my house and in my life.

We snuggled on the sofa to watch a movie. I relented and suffered through a chick flick, even handing her a tissue when the movie reduced her to tears. She watched and I thought. I thought of all the times she'd had to rush from a room to hide after a knock on the door; of all the times I'd had to leave after receiving a telephone call and all the times I'd played it cool in front of Joe. It had been a few months now, we were running on borrowed time before we were caught and I needed to make a plan. I wanted Joe to know.

"I need to take a shower," she said. I hadn't realised the movie had finished.

She left to head upstairs and the thought of her under the jets of the shower was just too tempting. I followed once I heard the water running.

I watched her soapy hands run over her body as I undressed. She shivered slightly when I opened the cubicle door and a blast of cold air ran over her skin. I pulled her to me, the water dripped down our faces, caught on our lips and our tongues as we kissed.

Evelyn ran her hands down my chest, down my stomach and clasped around my cock before lowering herself to her knees. She took me in her mouth, all the way to the back of her throat. To see her on her knees, to feel her mouth around my cock, and to see her looking back up at me while she sucked was pure pleasure. There was nothing submissive about her; she was totally in control. She brought me to the brink of release then slowed her pace; she had my heart pounding in my chest and calling out her name.

"Ev, I'm going to come," I said as I wrapped my fingers tighter in her hair.

I attempted to pull her away; instead she sucked harder, milking me, swallowing my come before releasing me from her mouth. I pulled her to her feet and my mouth crashed down on hers. I tasted myself on her tongue.

"Fuck me now," she said.

"I need a…"

She cut me off mid sentence. "No, you don't. I went on the pill."

I picked her up and she wrapped her legs around me waist. With one hand I slid open the cubicle door and rested her against the sink—I fucked her hard. Her screams filled the room as I teased her clitoris with my fingers, my cock still pounding while she came. She tightened around me, she clawed at my chest and I gripped so hard she would be left with an imprint of my hands.

Pulling out of her, I turned her around. She bent at the waist and I fucked her from behind. I wrapped my hand in her hair forcing her head up; I needed to watch her face, to see the emotion she felt. Sweat mixed with the cooling water on my skin, but inside I was on fire. I ached for her, I wanted to fuck her so hard she wouldn't walk after; I wanted to hear her scream out my name over and over. My release came hard and fast.

She rested her head down on the basin, both of us needing to get our breathing under control. I leant forward and placed a gentle kiss on her back.

"Wow," I whispered.

She giggled as I pulled out of her. I handed her some tissue to clean up with, doing the same myself. While she took another shower I made my way to the bedroom.

I was leaning against the open window with a cigarette and dressed just in jeans when she returned. I watched as she pulled on a pair of my shorts and a t-shirt and with a smile she left the room. I guessed I was always a little pensive after sex; it was mind-blowing and yet left me feeling sad. I was left sad because I wanted more. I wanted a relationship that was visible; I wanted her father to be proud that I was dating his daughter but that conversation always ran through my mind.

Joe wanted better than me for Evelyn and so he should.

****

Evelyn was busy in the kitchen when I entered; she was preparing dinner. I took some glasses from a cupboard, a bottle of wine and plates, and set them on the table. It felt so natural, so comfortable, to have her in my space and to have her cook me dinner.

"What do they all mean?" she asked as she joined me at the table.

"What?" I answered between mouthfuls of pasta.

"Your tattoos, do they have meanings?"

I'd added to my collection since being in America.

"Some, others are just designs I liked or drew myself. This one here," I said pointing to the dragon that snaked up my arm. "This one means strength and courage, something I needed a long time ago."

"Will you tell me about it?"

I set my fork down and rested back on my chair. She knew the basics, of course, but if I was to have the relationship I wanted with her, she needed to know the truth.

"It was a few days before I came here, to America, I think. I was with my sister in the square in my village. We were just watching the world go by when I saw him, one of the men that had taken my father and brother. I watched him sit with his friends, drinking coffee and laughing. I don't think I have ever felt such hatred; it was eating me up inside. His face was all I saw every time I closed my eyes. He caught me staring and I knew he thought there was something familiar about me but he couldn't place me. You know when someone frowns at you?"

I paused to take a sip of wine. All the while I had spoken, Evelyn's fingers had traced my tattoo.

"You don't have to tell me anymore, Rocco. It's fine," she whispered.

I needed to tell her, she needed to hear exactly what I had done. I recalled the rest of that evening. I had kept my eyes focused on the table until I came to end of my story.

"I stuck him right through his ribs, as far as I could. I imagine I punctured his lung and I watched him die," I said, looking at her as I spoke.

For a moment there was silence. "Oh, God," she said as she rushed to the sink.

As she retched I stood behind her holding her hair to one side and rubbed her back. I'd known that when she found out the truth she would be shocked; I had no idea it would be to the point of making her sick. I filled a glass of water and handed it to her.

"Sit, take a drink," I said quietly.

"I'm sorry, it was just a shock to hear you say that."

I shrugged my shoulders. "I haven't told anyone the full story. I ran, I left the girl there screaming and I ran home. The next thing, I was on a plane."

"What would have happened if you had stayed?"

"His friends came looking for me. You have to know, everyone knows everyone in the village. The girl must have described me well. Fucking amazing considering she was the one who went for him first," I tried to conceal the bitterness I still felt.

"If they had caught me, I would be dead," I added.

I searched her face for pity, for anger, for disgust even. There was sadness in her eyes but nothing more.

"As much as I respected your mother, I knew she didn't want me at your house. Your father thought it was the safest place. No one would come for me at your home. I didn't like it though. I was putting you at risk."

I turned to face her, her knees were between mine and I smoothed some hair from her face, tucking it behind her ear.

"I saw how you looked at me, I knew," I whispered. "I needed to get out, to protect you."

"Those men wouldn't have dared come to my house," she said.

"Not from them, from me. I was in a bad place."

She raised her hands and placed them either side of my face, her kiss was gentle at first. I stood and taking her hand, led her back to the bedroom. Silently I undressed her and then did the one thing I wanted so desperately to do—I made love to her.

With every part of my body, my mind and my soul, I made love to her.

Chapter Seven

I woke to the smell of coffee drifting up from the kitchen. I rolled to my side hugging the pillow that Evelyn had rested her head on to my chest. It smelt of her and I breathed in deep. Something had changed. The previous evening had been a turning point in our relationship and it scared me a little.

I rose and threw on a pair of jeans, pulled a t-shirt over my head before making my way downstairs. She was at the sink rinsing a cup when I wrapped my arms around her, she startled.

"I need to go out. Will you stay here?" I said.

"Now? It's so early," she said then laughed.

"I won't be long. Business."

She turned in my arms and kissed me hard, her hands fisted in my hair as she drew my head closer. Even as I sat in the car a few minutes later I could still taste her on my tongue.

****

I climbed the stairs to the office nodding at Paulo as I passed him sitting in his usual chair by the door.

"Rocco, come and sit. We have a problem," Joe said as I entered the office.

He was behind his desk with Jonathan to his side.

"What's up?"

"Geraldo called. It seems our friends have decided to reinstate their need for protection payment in the village."

I froze. "I need to get back."

"No, you need to stay here. I have it under control. I have an *associate* that is willing to help. The Commission are going to put measures in place to ensure our friends are no longer a threat to your family, but in the meantime, Geraldo wants your mother to stay with him and she's refusing."

I shook my head. "I'll talk to her, convince her to leave the farm."

"She's a stubborn woman, your mother. Talk to her today. But that's not the problem; there's a cost."

"What do you mean, a cost?"

"The Commission won't do anything without receiving something in return, you know that. This man needs to disappear."

Joe slid a photograph over the desk to me. I looked at the picture of an elderly man dressed in a blue suit. He was smiling for the camera. His face was familiar but I couldn't place where I'd seen him before.

"Who is he?"

"Senator Lukehurst, Greg Lukehurst."

I looked up at Joe. "You want me to get rid of a Senator?"

"Not me. I don't know the man, the Commission do. And not you personally. In return, they will rid the village of their troubles."

"Should I ask why?"

"No, not our business, Rocco. We have been asked to assist in this matter because the Senator lives in Washington. I want you to meet someone tomorrow."

"You don't trust me to do the hit?"

"Oh, I do, Rocco. But you are too important to me if things go wrong. Tomorrow you meet Tony, he has *special skills*, shall we say."

Joe chuckled and Jonathan furrowed his brow. I'd heard the name before but never met the man. He was reclusive. No one knew where he lived but he could be called upon if the hit was high profile or likely to be real messy.

"Okay, let me know where and when and I'll be there. You want me to keep this?" I said, holding the photograph.

"No, that stays here. I want you to organise but no more. Believe me, you don't want to be around when Tony gets to work. The Senator has information the Commission requires, this isn't a straight hit."

Joe left, taking Paulo with him, after that conversation. I walked him to his car before returning to the office.

"What do you make of that?" I asked Jonathan.

"Taking out a Senator is pretty big business. He must have some serious information if the Commission want him dead."

There had been a spate of arrests in New York. The FBI were trialling a new set of laws, laws that meant a whole family could be arrested for the same crime regardless of who the perpetrator was. That's when it dawned on me where I'd seen the Senator before. He had been the one who drew up the bill and place it before congress.

"He proposed the new Rico laws, didn't he?" I said, more to myself.

"Yes, I guess that's why he's not popular right now. Now, what's going on with Evelyn?"

"She's over at my house. I should get back," I said as I rose from my chair.

After saying goodbye, I headed back to my car and drove home. It was a beautiful day, the sun was shining and a warm breeze blew in from the open window. I lit a cigarette and thoughts of the Senator left my mind, replaced by a naked Evelyn.

****

"Ciao," I called out as I saw her sitting in the yard.

She rose to greet me and her smile was infectious. "Let me get you a coffee."

"Mmm, I could get used to this," I said as I took off my t-shirt and sat on the metal chair.

Evelyn brought me a coffee and sat opposite with her book.

"What are you reading?" I asked.

She showed me the cover. "Knights on white horses and all that shit, huh?"

"It's romance, Rocco, something us girls love."

I chuckled. "Well, come on over here. You can always ride me."

Evelyn laughed as she climbed onto my lap, her knees were either side of my legs and she wrapped her hands around my shoulders.

"You are so beautiful," I mumbled into her neck.

I kissed my way up her throat, feeling her pulse quicken under my lips.

"It's been good having you here and sleeping in my bed," I said.

"I know, I don't want to leave."

"Maybe it's time, Evelyn, we tell your father. You can move in with me."

"My father won't let me move in with you even if he did approve of us," she replied.

"We'll see. There's something going on right now though. I can't tell you but in a week or so, I'll talk to him."

I saw the look of alarm that crossed her face.

"Your father is fine. It's just business that needs to be concluded. He will be in a happy place after, trust me."

As Evelyn settled into my lap a loud knock could be heard from the front door. I jumped from the chair and raised my fingers to my lips. She nodded as I pointed to a corner in the yard and pulled on my t-shirt. Opening the door I saw Jonathan and his new love, Patricia.

"Hey, give you a fright, did I?" he said with a laugh.

"Yeah, you could have called ahead."

I stepped to one side allowing Jonathan and Patricia to enter. Before I'd even got to the kitchen I watched Jonathan open the back door and peer out.

"Want a glass of wine, Evelyn?" he said.

"You scared me, again," she said as she stepped from the shadow.

He laughed and made his way to the small table, followed by Patricia. I grabbed some glasses and a bottle before joining them.

"Evelyn, may I introduce Patricia," Jonathan said.

"Hi, I'm really glad to meet you," Patricia held out her hand to Evelyn.

"Joe doesn't know Evelyn is dating Rocco, so no mention of her being here, okay?" Jonathan said gently.

After pouring wine, I sat beside Ev, my arm rested on the back of her chair. We chatted for an hour or so, drinking wine and soaking up the last of the day's rays before the sun disappeared on the horizon.

"Ev, I think your father is expecting you back for dinner," Jonathan said as he drained the last of his wine.

Our perfect weekend was coming to a close. It would be better for Jonathan to take Evelyn home; he lived close by. It was Sunday evening; there was no doubt Joe would be at home. An evening meal with all the family every Sunday was all Joe insisted of his children.

I followed Evelyn upstairs to pack her bag. Standing in the bedroom with the bed still unmade, I sighed. I lifted her chin so her eyes, brimming with tears, could meet mine.

"It's been a perfect weekend, Evelyn. Thank you."

The kiss she returned was fierce and wanting. We were breathless when we pulled apart.

"I'll see you in a couple of days?" she whispered, her voice catching.

"Of course."

I watched as the car drove away and Evelyn looked out the rear view window. Just before the car turned the corner she blew a kiss.

"I love you," I mouthed, not knowing if she understood.

I loved her, heart and soul, and as soon as the Senator was taken care of I was going to speak to Joe. I would prove to him I was worthy of her, I would marry her and he could be proud of me.

It was the last time I ever kissed her and the last time I held her in my arms.

Chapter Eight

The following day Joe, Paulo and I drove to Fredrico's. The restaurant was empty save for one man sitting in a corner booth nursing a coffee. I guessed him to be a little older than me but it was hard to tell. He wore a black suit, a white shirt and had the most startling cold blue eyes. He rose and gave a broad smile as we approached.

"Tony, please, sit. I'd like to introduce you to Rocco," Joe said as we joined Tony at the table.

"Rocco, I've heard many things about you. It's good to finally meet you."

We shook hands and he had a firm grip, which surprised me. He was slight in build but had strength. I guessed his suit hid an athletic body.

Fredrico brought over more coffee and Joe slid the photograph of the Senator towards Tony.

"What do you need?" Tony asked.

"The Senator seems to be playing two sides. He has knowledge of a murder that my friend in New York wants to ensure never gets shared. They would like to know the name of his contact in the FBI. It's believed this bill he's proposing is so he can take down my friend and protect himself."

"Okay, straight forward enough. Usual deal?" Tony asked.

"Of course, you will be paid on completion, normal way."

"So where do you fit in?" Tony turned to me as he spoke.

"As you know, the Senator won't be an easy target. It was proposed that perhaps Rocco could arrange to meet with him, on the pretence of an exchange of information. This pig, he knows us, he doesn't know you. You would never get close enough. Rocco arranges the meet; you'll need extra firepower as he won't be coming alone. You then do what you do best," Joe answered.

That was the first I'd heard of the plan to abduct and ultimately kill the Senator.

"The Senator won't come heavily guarded, he won't run the risk of too many people seeing him with Rocco. I'll provide the cars, the guns and the men. They will hand him over to you and then their job is done," Joe added.

"Do we have a timeframe?" Tony asked.

"This needs to be done soon, before this bill is passed. I have no idea what your schedule is like, Tony, but I'm asking as a favour that this is done tomorrow evening."

"My surgery is available whenever you are ready," he replied.

As he said the word *surgery* he grinned, perfectly straight white teeth were displayed yet his smile never reached his eyes. He was one scary fucker for sure.

"Rocco, you make contact then you get in touch. I'll be waiting," Tony said, then rose and strode out of the restaurant.

I turned to Joe. "So how do I make contact with a fucking Senator?"

I was a little pissed to have been told the plan in that way. I would have liked to discuss it with Joe before meeting Dr. Death as I called him.

"It's all been done, Rocco. The Senator believes that you are representing our friend from New York. You're to meet him here tomorrow night. The restaurant will be closed, he'll come with two security, one normally stays by the car, the other will follow him in. I'd take out the one by the car first. The Senator is a cocky fucker. He believes he's untouchable and that makes him arrogant but careless. I can't trust anyone but you to pull this off, Rocco."

"So who do I have with me?"

"Mack, of course—you need the muscle—and Paulo. Paulo can drive the Senator's car and deliver him to Tony. At that point, Rocco, you leave. Do not stay around."

I nodded. As much as I had no issue with killing someone, the thought of what Dr. Death was capable of turned my stomach.

"His security will be armed of course, so deal with them quickly. Fredrico will spike our Senator's coffee with a little extra something. He'll be out before you know it."

I nodded and a plan formed in my mind. "Is the Senator usually armed?"

"I would imagine for this he would be. Just don't get shot, okay?"

I shook my head and sighed. Joe smiled, that was all in a day's work for him and I wondered if Evelyn really had any idea what her father was capable of. I had no idea of the name of the *friend*; it was Joe's way. No one person knew everything, that strategy protected him and us.

We stood and made our way back to the car.

****

I met with Mack later in the day and discussed my plan. Richard was sent to find me an address. A distraction was required and I knew exactly what that was going to be.

It was an hour later that I stood outside an apartment in a block that seriously needed some attention. The sound of a child crying could be heard through the front door. I knocked and waited. I listened to the sound of multiple bolts being released before the door opened a fraction, a chain only allowing it to open so far.

"Nina, do you remember me?" I asked.

She nodded. "I do, and I guess you've come to be *thanked* for covering the rent."

She held in her arms a blond child; he looked at me with fearful eyes and a snotty nose. His clothes were clean and he looked well cared for but something had clearly distressed him.

"I've come to offer you a job, and not the kind of job you're thinking of. Can I come in?"

She thought for a moment before closing the door and releasing the chain. The child had stopped his crying and as I entered the apartment, she sat him on the sofa. He cuddled a blanket close to him as he sucked on his thumb.

"Cute kid," I said and smiled at him.

"I'm sorry for being abrupt. I'm not used to being helped. I should thank you," she replied.

"You deserved it. Sit, I want to talk to you."

Nina sat on the sofa closest to her child and to show respect I sat in a chair on the opposite side of the small living room. The apartment was clean and tidy, sparsely furnished with what looked like second-hand furniture but comfortable. In one corner was a desk piled high with books; school books.

"Do you know who I am?" I asked.

"I know your name is Rocco and I know who Sammy is...was...so I guess you work together?"

"Sammy worked for me. I'd like to offer you a one-time job. You will earn enough money to pay your way through college without having to *work*."

"I was always told, Rocco, that if something sounds too good, it usually is. I guess I have to sell my soul here."

I chuckled and nodded slightly. "Selling your soul is part of the deal. Well, assuring me of your silence would be more appropriate."

"What if I can't offer that?"

"Then I walk away and you'll hear no more from me."

I reached into my jacket pocket and pulled out a stack of bills. There had to be close to a thousand dollars. It was more money that she would make in a year selling her body and would certainly cover her college fees.

"That is a down payment. Accept my offer and you will receive a little more."

"What if I take your money and run?"

"Then you make your child an orphan."

She stared at me and swallowed hard. I didn't want to frighten her just lay down the facts.

"You can't run from me. I will find you. I'm not trying to scare you but you need to know who you are dealing with before you open your smart mouth again."

"What do I have to do?" she whispered, her eyes fixed on the money.

"It's real simple. I have to meet a man, he has a driver that I'd like you to distract."

"You want me to fuck him? You said your *job…*"

I cut her off. "Did I say I wanted you to fuck him? I'm not a pimp, Nina. I'm giving you a way out of that life. I've paid your fucking rent for a year. I want you to distract him, lure him away from a car. You fall over, you bat your pretty eyelashes at him, I don't care how, you just get him away from the car."

"And then what?"

"And then an associate will take over and you go home."

"That's all?"

"That's all, except, breathe a word to anyone and like I said earlier, your kid becomes an orphan. Do you have family, Nina? Is there anyone who could care for him long term?"

She shook her head as she pulled him close to her chest.

"Then don't risk him being sent to an orphanage. Kids aren't treated so well there. Do as I ask and you'll have enough money to pay for college, get a great job and move on with your life."

I was taking a gamble. She could run, skip town, but there was something about her that assured me she wouldn't. She was a good woman just trying to make it in life.

"Can I trust you, Nina?" I asked.

She took a moment before nodding. "Yes, you can trust me."

"Good. Someone will collect you at eight o'clock tomorrow evening. You can get a sitter I take it?"

"Yeah, Macy downstairs can care for him. So I just have to fall over and hope this guys comes to help me, right?"

"Right."

"And if he doesn't?"

"Call out to him, make him, Nina. If you have done all you can to distract him and he ignores you, fine, you keep that money and get on with your life. Get him away from the car and you'll get another payment."

"Are you going to kill him?" Her voice had quieted.

"No, do I look like a killer to you?"

She didn't answer. I stood and buttoned up my jacket. "Tomorrow, Nina. Be ready for eight."

Part one of my plan was in place and I headed back to the office.

"Paulo, you pick up a woman called Nina at this address tomorrow, eight o'clock sharp. Take her to Fredrico's. She'll distract our driver then you put a bullet in his skull. Put the girl in the car and wait for me and the Senator, okay?" I handed over the address.

"Nina?"

"Yeah, the girl Sammy roughed up."

"Okay, can we trust her?"

"Yes. Mack, you need to take out the Senator's guy as soon as his coffee starts to take effect. We won't have much time, while the Senator is drowsy, we get him to the car."

It was a simple plan but one that could go wrong on so many levels. Timing was going to be crucial.

I checked my watch. I had wanted to see Evelyn but Joe had plans for a family meal out and I had to focus. A lot was riding on that job; my family's security, my reputation and Joe's trust. If I pulled it off, I believed Joe would be proud and, I hoped, more open to my relationship with his daughter. I headed for home.

The house was quiet and Evelyn's perfume still lingered. It pleased me to have her scent in my home. She had left a cardigan on the arm of the sofa and I raised it to my face. The soft fabric brushed against my cheek as I inhaled. I was reminded of the time I had caught her doing the same thing a few years previous.

I sat in the kitchen thinking of Evelyn. She would be twenty years old in a few days. I had known her since she was sixteen, watched her blossom into a woman and the past months that we had been secretly meeting had been some of the best of my life.

I slept well that night despite the task I was to undertake the following evening and despite the bed feeling way too large with just my body on it.

One weekend was all it took for my house to feel empty without her, for my bed to feel cold and for me to miss her.

****

The weather reflected my mood; it was cold, rain fell heavily, flooding the sidewalk. Dark ominous clouds blocked out the moonlight as I stopped the car outside Fredrico's. There was no doubt the Senator would have sent someone to scout the place already and Fredrico would have played his part well. The spanner in the works was the weather; I was banking on a clear night so the driver of the car wouldn't need to be wrapped up inside it. I only hoped there was a gentleman lurking under the suit and armour.

"Rocco, sit over here. Can I get you a coffee?" Fredrico asked as I entered.

"Sure, a normal one though, yeah?"

He raised his eyebrows and smirked. "Of course, my friend. A coffee for you too, Mack?"

Mack stood a little away from the table. The Senator would know I wouldn't be alone, he would also assume the information I had to give him wouldn't be divulged in front of anyone.

Senator Lukehurst believed he was meeting with me to be told the family behind the recent killing of the Chief of Police in NY. He would then offer that information to his FBI pals, a whole family would be removed from the street and his bill proves to have worked. It gets passed; he gets a Presidential pat on the back and slithers further up the political ladder. Truth was, I had no idea who took out the Chief of Police, and neither did I care. What I did care about was that I was being used as a pawn in a game between families.

While I sipped my coffee and waited, I pondered. I might have come from simple farmers but I wasn't a dumb man. My gut instinct was screaming that either Joe or me was about to be set up. My senses were on high alert.

The door opened and a gust of wind blew through the restaurant. I stood to greet my guest. As predicted one man shadowed the Senator. He was carrying under his jacket; the bulge of a handgun could be clearly seen by his breast pocket.

"Senator," I said as he approached.

"Rocco, it's great to finally meet you. I've been following your progress," he replied, a veiled admission that he was keeping an eye on me.

"Likewise, Senator. It's always nice to have *friends* that are connected, wouldn't you say?"

He was a cocky fucker; to the point that when he removed his jacket before sitting, he also removed a handgun he had been concealing and placed it on the table next to his hand. If I was supposed to be scared, he'd need to do more than that.

"Senator, you insult me. Here I was about to give you some valuable information, to help your cause, eliminate *your* problem and you bring a gun to our meeting."

"One can never be too careful, Rocco, and I don't trust you wops."

"Mmm, interesting choice of words. I'd be careful, Senator. There are two of you and four of us *wops* as you call us. Are the odds in your favour?"

Mack stepped forward from his resting place in the corner of the room, Fredrico returned with a coffee in his hand and a shotgun over his shoulder, the chef, someone who's name I never knew, stepped from the kitchen. The front of his white tunic was covered in blood. I wanted to laugh; I had no idea if that was for effect or if he had been feeding the dogs.

The Senator's security immediate went for his gun.

"Now, let's all relax shall we? Here, Senator, have a coffee, on the house. Or would you prefer wine? I have a wonderful Merlot that's recently been flown in," Fredrico said.

The Senator shook his head at his guy who relaxed a little.

"Coffee smells good," he said as he took a sip. I noticed the very slight shake to his hand.

"Now, shall we get back to business?" he asked as he drained the rest of his drink.

"Of course."

Sitting on the table was a plain white envelope and I slid it towards the Senator. He looked at it for a few moments before loosening his tie. Beads of sweat appeared on his forehead and upper lip. The timing was perfect. Just as he was about to speak I heard a car open slam and then a woman scream. Security number two reached for his gun but at the same time turned towards the restaurant door. I swiped the Senators gun from the table; the sound of metal hitting the tiled floor had the security spinning back towards us. He was too late. Mack stepped forward and shot him through his temple.

"What the fuck…?" the Senator said, his voice raspy.

"Mack, do you know how many times I've had to replace those curtains?" Fredrico said as he strode into the restaurant, the chef following.

Blood had spattered over the window and across the floral curtains, curtains that were already in need of replacing in my opinion. The chef grabbed the security guy by the feet and dragged him through the restaurant, a trail of smeared blood followed.

"He's fucking US Capitol Police," the Senator said.

"He could be Secret Service for all I care. Did you really think you could take on the family you have?" I shook my head as he struggled to keep his eyes open.

"Time to go," I called out to Mack.

Even with us either side of the Senator it was hard going. He was a dead weight as we dragged him to the car. Paulo was sitting up front and as we approached he unlocked the door. At the same time Nina tried to climb out.

"You fucking liar, you told me no one was going to get killed. He shot that man, fucking shot him in front of me," she screamed as her fists rained down on my chest.

I let go of the Senator and pushed Nina back in the car.

"Calm the fuck down. We're taking you home."

"You lied to me."

"No I never. You asked me if I was going to kill someone, did I?"

"What's up with him?"

"He's drunk and we are taking him home too. Now sit down."

I climbed in the car next to Nina who scooted as far away as possible, her body was pressed against the side of the car and she kept her head facing the window. Mack positioned the Senator alongside me.

We drove in silence for a while until we hit a stoplight. Nina tugged on the door handle.

"It won't open from the inside, Nina. Not until the driver releases the lock. You are not in any danger. I promised that you would walk away with a shitload of money and you'd never see me again, providing you keep your mouth shut," I said.

She had started to cry.

"I wouldn't have agreed to this. He fucking shot him," she said through her sobs.

"The man he shot, Nina, wasn't a good man. He hurt some children, children as young as your son. You want him on the streets?" I lied.

We fell silent as we made our way through the city. Once into Columbia Heights, Paulo pulled the car over outside Nina's apartment block.

"You lured a man to his death, Nina, that makes you an accomplice. As I said, keep your mouth shut and this is the last time you will see me, understand?"

She nodded her head before the door was released and she left. Paulo pulled back into the traffic and on to our next destination. It was a short drive back out into Great Falls, and to a farm secluded amongst woodland. Passing the house, we carried on up a dirt path to an outbuilding. Tony was waiting for us.

The Senator groaned as we manhandled him from the car; he had started to come round. Despite his slight build, Tony was as strong as Mack and heaved the Senator inside. I stopped at the door stunned by what I saw. It was indeed a *surgery*. An IV was set up next to a metal gurney in the centre of the room. A tray of surgical instruments stood to one side and, bizarrely, classical music played. The Senator was forced onto the gurney, his arms and legs strapped to hold him there. Tony turned and smiled at me before gesturing to the door. It was time for me to leave.

Paulo pulled up outside the office to let me out, his last job was to get rid of the car. I climbed the stairs to be met by Joe.

"How did it go?" he asked. Mack had already returned so I guessed he knew.

"Fine, job done. The Senator is with Tony."

"The girl?"

"She's trustworthy. She's the girl Sammy fucked over."

"Good, now we have another problem. Sit down."

I didn't like the tone of his voice, nor the look on his face, as he asked me to sit.

"There's trouble at home; your sister has disappeared. I'm still waiting for full details. It may have been nothing."

I jumped from my chair. "Have we been double crossed?"

"No, I'm confident our friends will follow through on their promise. This could just be coincidence."

"I need to get home. Just for a couple of days."

"I don't think that's wise, Rocco. Geraldo is capable…"

I cut him off mid sentence. "Geraldo is an old man, Joe. If my family is in danger, I want to be there."

"You could be over-reacting, wait until we know more."

"No. Jonathan, run me to the airport. I'll get a ticket when I get there."

"Rocco, wait. We don't know how safe it is for you yet," Joe said.

"Then I suggest, Joe, you get on the phone to your *friends*. I've held up my end, now they need to step up."

Joe sagged a little in his chair; he looked distressed.

"I'll be fine, Joe. Two days and I'll be back."

Jonathan and I headed down to one of the cars. We arrived at my home and with the engine still running I ran to find my passport. I didn't pack any clothes—all I wanted to do was to get to the airport and board a flight. I had no idea if there would be even be a flight available but I had to try.

"Will you do me a favour? Don't tell Evelyn if she asks. Just tell her I'll be back soon. I don't want her worrying," I told Jonathan.

"I don't think this is the right thing, Rocco. But if she asks, I'll tell you had to go away on business," he replied.

I nodded my thanks as I left the car and walked into the airport. The only flight leaving that night was to the UK; I booked a seat. I'd figure out how to get to Rome from there. Sitting in a coffee house, I stared at a bank of telephones along one wall. Should I call her? I desperately wanted to hear Evelyn's voice, I hadn't spoken to her for two days and I knew she would be worried. Before I could make my mind up, my flight was called. I'd ring as soon as I returned home.

Chapter Nine

It took two days to get to Rome. Two fucking days of sitting in airports and arguing with check-in staff because I had no luggage. Finally, I found myself at a car rental desk about to pick up keys and then I was on my way. The drive to the village took a couple of hours and as I wound down the window letting the heat of the summer blow through I started to relax.

Stopping at a service station for gas, I called Geraldo. He was annoyed that I had made the journey; it appeared the *trouble* was a simple car accident that Adriana had been involved in. She had never learnt to drive but had taken the old truck out late one night to meet a new boyfriend. Mamma had panicked, seeing her empty bedroom had her thinking she had been abducted. Adriana was found sitting beside the truck the following morning. Joe had called Geraldo to inform him I was on my way but it was too late for anyone to contact me.

"Rocco," I heard as I climbed from the car.

Mamma came running from the orchard as soon as she saw me. She wrapped her arms around me and it shocked me to see how frail she had become. Although we had spoken, I hadn't seen her in four years. Tears streamed down her cheeks but to see the smile on her face made the journey worthwhile.

"Look at you. My son, you're a man now."

"Mamma, I was a man when I left," I replied with a laugh.

"I bet you're hungry. Let me feed you."

Placing my arm around her shoulder, I led her into the house. Mamma liked to feed people, and by feed I meant, at a moment's notice a banquet could be prepared. It wasn't long after that Geraldo arrived.

"Rocco, you didn't need to come. Your sister caused so much fuss but it's good to see you," he said.

"I'll be having words with her later. Where is she?"

"She was sent for some supplies. It might be time to find her a husband, someone who can control her ways."

"Yeah, well, good luck with that," I replied laughing.

Mamma, Geraldo and I sat outside to eat. Plates of meats, cheese, olives and the ripest tomatoes were laid out. It felt a little strange to be back. It was the first time in four years I'd spoken my native language and I laughed at Mamma's confused look when I added a few 'Americanisms'.

****

I thought of Evelyn, of what was going to be when I returned. I knew the minute I landed I was going to speak with Joe. I wanted him to know how much I loved his daughter. I tore a piece of paper from a pad and finding a pen, I began to write my thoughts. Those thoughts turned into a letter I guessed.

I didn't tell you, but I do love you, Evelyn, and I will tell you that every day and more. I don't know why I am writing this; I don't think I'll ever give it you. I'm just writing my thoughts, preparing for when I see you next. I want it all straight in my head when I ask your father for his blessing to marry you. I picture that day; you will be beautiful and you will be mine.

I'll be the proudest man, watching you walk on your father's arm to be handed over to me.

I'm sitting among the olive trees imagining you here, our children playing in the grass. This is something that will always be a dream though. Perhaps, later, who knows. I want a daughter, Evelyn. I want a daughter who will look just like you, and then a son and I will cherish them. I'll work hard; we can start our own business, a safe one and buy a house. I want that life so much it hurts.

You gave me the ultimate gift—yourself. I hear your moans in my head when my hands touched you and all I want to do is lay next to you holding you in my arms. I want to feel your skin, so smooth and so soft. I want to stroke your hair and kiss your lips. I want, well, you know what I want.

I'll be home tomorrow and the first thing I'm going to do is find you. I don't care who knows. I love you. I want everyone to know that. I LOVE YOU.

I folded the piece of paper and headed to my old bedroom. The time difference and heat of summer had worn me out. I wanted to take a nap before telling my mother that I would be leaving the following morning. She would be upset at the shortness of my visit but I needed to get back to Evelyn. My mind was made up. No matter what Joe thought, I would be marrying Evelyn. She would carry my children. We would have the dream we both wanted.

****

The following morning, after eating enough breakfast to last the day, I said my goodbyes. Adriana couldn't quite meet my eyes; I had torn a strip off her the previous evening when she had finally returned. Mamma cried and Geraldo shook my hand. I backed the car up the dusty drive and with one last look in the rear view mirror I headed off.

I guess I wasn't paying attention as I drove; I was absorbed in the smells of the countryside that wafted through the window. From the corner of my eye I caught sight of a silver car as it tried to overtake me. The road wasn't wide enough for it to pass safely so I slowed a little. As I did, I saw the driver smirk at me before he turned his steering wheel hard. The squeal of metal scraping against metal set my teeth on edge.

"What the fuck?" I called out, trying to keep my car on the road.

He did it again. I fought with the wheel as my car swerved towards the edge of the road, its wheels kicking up dust and stones as we left the tarmac. I tried hard to keep the car on the road but it was useless. The wheels spun on the dirt losing traction. The steering wheel was wrenched from my hands and the car rolled down the bank running alongside the road.

Metal crunched, glass shattered and I was thrown around the car like a rag doll. It finally came to rest on its roof. I was dazed and my head pounded. I heard a groan, it took a moment to realise that the sound had come from me. I stretched out my legs expecting to feel pain and was amazed to not. I moved my arm and a searing pain shot through my shoulder. The smell of burning had started to fill the car and I knew I had to move. I crawled through the open window and rolled away.

I was on my back looking up at the blue sky trying to process what had happened. I remembered a silver car then the countryside tumbling around me. As my brain came into focus, the sunlight was blotted out. A shadow loomed over me and I was dragged by my arms back up the bank.

I screamed out in pain as my shoulder was wrenched from its socket and I passed out.

****

Cold water hit my face and I spluttered. My eyes opened and I found myself sitting in an office and looking at an older man sitting opposite me. Between us was a small table.

"Rocco, good to see you're awake," he said.

"Where the fuck am I?" I asked.

"All in good time. I'm sorry my guys were a little heavy handed; they will be punished for that. I just wanted to talk to you. You see, you've caused me some problems. I am missing a Senator."

"I don't know what you mean."

"You do, Rocco. I might not be a fancy American but don't insult my intelligence."

"Since you appear to know who I am, you'll also know I work to orders. The Commission instructed the disappearance of the Senator."

"Fuck your Commission. They have no control here," he replied.

At that point I knew I was in trouble. Any family working outside the Commission were on the outside for a reason—they were not wanted nor were they trusted. Had I been set up? Had Joe sold me out?

"I appear to have forgotten my manners. Rocco, let me offer you a coffee at least."

I shook my head. "Whatever *plans* you have for me, let's just get on with it, shall we? I don't really feel the need to be sociable. You had my fucking car ran off the road, I'm dragged by these pricks to be sat in front of you and for what? You got a problem with a missing Senator, take it up with the Commission."

I was fucking angry. I felt something hard and cold press against my temple, the clicking sound told me a gun was pressed to my head, primed and ready to fire.

"Now, now. Rocco, I don't have *plans* for you, not in the way you think anyway. I just want your help. That's not too much to ask, is it?"

"That depends on what help you want."

The gun was removed from my head and a coffee was placed alongside a large envelope on the small table. He leant forwards and picked up the envelope.

"I want to know who ordered the hit on the Senator."

"You think I'd know that?" I said with a bitter laugh.

"No, but I do believe you have the skills to find out. I know it wasn't your Guiseppi and I also know it wasn't the idiots causing trouble in your village. Those idiots will be taken care of, by the way. At least that end of the deal is being upheld."

"You seem to know a lot," I said. One thought ran through my mind. *Who the fuck is this guy?*

"I know Guiseppi was asked, in return for your villagers safety, to take out the Senator and I want to know why and by whom."

"I don't know by *whom*. All I do know is the Senator had information that wasn't to be made public."

There seemed no point in lying; I was fucked either way. I watched as he picked up the enveloped and slid out what looked like a photograph. He smiled as he studied it.

"Such a pretty girl, be a shame to scar that body," he said as he threw the photograph down on the table.

It was a black and white picture of my sister. I closed my eyes not wanting to see the image of her naked body lying on a bed, smiling at whoever was taking the shot, but I had. I gritted my teeth together and my hands gripped the arms of the chair I was sat on.

But it was the next photograph that sealed my fate, that destroyed my dreams for a future and I tried desperately not to show any emotion.

"If you want her to live, you'd be wise to do as I require." He slowly placed a photograph of Evelyn on top of the one of my sister.

She had her face raised to the sun as she sat on the steps of the church. I remembered the day, I was running a little late to collect her. She wore the white summer dress with the red flowers. She was smiling; she was happy.

"Evelyn is another pretty girl. How did you manage to fuck her, huh?"

I sprang from my chair and kicked over the table before arms wrapped around my chest and forced me back down.

"You lay one filthy hand on her and you know there will be a fucking war," I spat.

"See, now you insult me again. What do you think will happen when someone realises you didn't make it home, huh? You were involved in a car accident, your body—well, a body—will be found in that burnt out wreck. Your Mamma will bury you, your family will mourn for you and no one will know any different. You think I can't make the precious Evelyn disappear and it look like an accident?"

My heart was pounding in my chest, my palms sweated as the anger built up inside me. I fought back tears—tears of pain and tears of anger. My heart shattered with the realisation that, yes, he could make her disappear.

"What do you want from me?" I asked, defeated.

"You work with me, Rocco. I will gain your trust and in time you will realise that this is a wonderful opportunity for you. You'll live in a luxurious house in Rome; you will have money, lots of it, cars, women and the finest handmade clothes until you deliver me the family that ordered the Senator's killing. Then you are free to leave if you should wish to."

"On one condition: I talk to Evelyn, I explain."

He shook his head and sighed. "Now you know that won't ever happen. You speak to her, she's dead; you flee, she's dead. One whisper that you have made contact with anyone in America, with your family even, she's dead. You see, Rocco, to those people you are already dead."

He rose from his chair and buttoned his jacket. "Tonight, you rest. I'll have someone look at that shoulder for you. In the morning I want your answer."

"And if I say no?"

"Then she's dead." He walked away.

****

I was driven to a hotel, a very upmarket hotel and shown to a suite on the top floor. My mind was in turmoil. I still didn't know his name but got that he was from Rome. There were some powerful families in Rome. My knowledge of Costa Nostra was limited to the families in America but I knew there were far more powerful ones in Italy. It seemed I had just landed myself in a heap load of shit with one of them.

I lay on the bed fully clothed and realised I had no choice. Adriana, Mamma, Geraldo, everyone would think I was dead and if I made contact, I had no doubt Evelyn would be. For the first time in a while I let the tears fall. I buried my face in the pillow knowing there was someone outside the door and quietly cried.

I cried for Evelyn, for the children we would never have. I cried for my Mamma having to bury her 'son' when I was still alive. I cried for myself. I was fucked—big time. I would do what he asked. I would do anything to ensure the safety of my family and Evelyn and I vowed, one day, I would kill him.

Letter from Rocco

I made a decision that day to walk away from the only woman I ever loved. The only woman I wanted to marry, to father her children and to grow old with. I believed in my heart she would die if I didn't and I could never live with the knowledge that I had been responsible for that. I prayed night after night that she would grieve then move on. That she would meet a wonderful man worthy of her, marry and live happy.

I moved to Rome and I worked for Salvatore Beneditti, head of a powerful family and the Ndrangheto.

Salvatore got the information he required. I wasn't released from his employment immediately, it took a few years and then I did return to America, briefly. I saw Evelyn from a distance; I also saw her wearing an engagement ring. I was pleased for her but I was too damaged by the things I had done and the things I had left to do to make a life with her. I had killed many.

I am a powerful man; I am now the head of a powerful family and the Ndrangheto. Even more so after overthrowing the Sicilian Costa Nostra and the Naples Camorra. I am the head of the most powerful crime organisation in the world, according to the press.

At heart, I am a simple farmer's son who loved so desperately and lost.

It's that loss that drives me to do all that I have and one day, soon, I'll have achieved everything I set out to do and then, who knows? Maybe I can find that dream again.

My name is Rocco and this is my story. It isn't over yet.

Acknowledgements

I could never have written the Fallen Angel series without the support of my family. My husband has been my rock, without him, I wouldn't be here.

My heartfelt thanks to the best beta readers a girl could want, Karen Shenton, Alison Parkins, Lucii Grubb and Rebecca Sherwin - your input is invaluable.

Thank you to Margreet Asslebergs of Rebel Edit & Design for yet another wonderful cover.

I'd also like to give a huge thank you to my editor - Megan Gunter with Indie Solutions by Murphy Rae. Please check out their web site - www.murphyrae.net

A hug goes out to the guys in Tracie's Fallen Angels, a fan page on Facebook - you cheer me up and give me reason to keep writing.

An even bigger hug goes to the ladies in my team. These ladies give up their time to support and promote my books. Karen Shenton, Louise White, Louise Bailey, Lilian Flesher, Jennifer Teasley Bruno, Angel Parkinson, Lucii Grubb, Kerry-Ann Bell and Lindsey Poage Norwood.

To all the wonderful bloggers that been involved in promoting my books and joining tours, thank you and I appreciate your support. There are too many to name individually – you know who you are.

To my research guru who shall remain nameless – thank you for your advice, for listening to my plot ideas and guiding me with procedures.

I am fortunate to have made many friends in the book world, some wonderful authors that I've met on my journey and I now class as close friends, book besties if you will. Rebecca Sherwin, Ava Manello and K L Shandwick – you ladies rock, big time! Your support and encouragement, your willingness to share ideas and just talk 'books' is precious to me, thank you. I urge you to check out these ladies – they write some amazing books.

If you wish to keep up to date with information on this series and future releases - and have the chance to enter monthly competitions, feel free to sign up for my newsletter. You can find the details on my web site:

www.TraciePodger.com

Turn your face to the sun and the shadow falls behind you.

About the Author

Tracie Podger currently lives in Kent, UK with her husband and a rather obnoxious cat called George. She's a Padi Scuba Diving Instructor with a passion for writing. Tracie has been fortunate to have dived some of the wonderful oceans of the world where she can indulge in another hobby, underwater photography. She likes getting up close and personal with sharks.

Tracie wishes to thank you for giving your time to read her books and hopes you enjoy them as much as she loves writing them. If you would like to know more, please feel free to contact her, she would love to hear from you.

Twitter: @Tracie Podger

Facebook: Tracie Podger, Author

www.TraciePodger.com

Available in ebook and paperback...

Fallen Angel, Part 1

Fallen Angel, Part 2

Fallen Angel, Part 3

Evelyn - A Novella

Rocco – A Novella

Robert

Travis

Coming soon....

Fallen Angel, Part 4

A Virtual Affair

The Passion Series

The Twisted Series

by

Rebecca Sherwin

Life is unpredictable. It can throw us happiness, luck, wealth and success at any given time, without warning or premonition. But it can also send trauma, trials and surprises, both unexpected and unwelcome.

The Twisted series explores a world where happiness is chased but unreachable, life is found and stolen, and love is fought for and sacrificed.

It is not a simple story – life is not a fairytale.

Sometimes it's a fight for Survival…

Survival

With intertwining memories and a world of deceit and betrayal yet to be exposed, Survival, book #1 in the Twisted series, is an intense, compelling page-turner, seen through the eyes of Skye 'the Skillet' Jones.

A mother. A father. Two daughters and a son. A happy suburban family of five.

An alcoholic mother. An absent father.

Abandonment. A family ripped apart.

Oliver. Beautiful Oliver. My twin brother, my protector.

Fighting. Freedom. Death.

Cut Throat Curtis. My fire and ice. My light and shade. My pleasure and pain.

He taught me to fight; to control emotional turmoil with physical distraction. He had pain of his own, secrets he would never reveal, and I should have known it would only be a matter of time until he left, becoming a ghost in a life I no longer knew.

Thomas. My magic. My fairy-tale. The man who promised the happy ever after I'd never dared to dream of. My prince. My lover. My everything and more.

But fate was waiting, as always. The merciless force of kismet watched over me, biding its time, waiting to strike; to plunge me into the depths of defeat and leave me with no choice but to succumb.

It was coming, the twist of fate that would bring me to my knees. It was up to me, Skye the Skillet, to decide whether to bow down and surrender to its will, or fight back, to fight for what I had left.

To fight for my survival…

Chapter One

I had the perfect life. No, really, I did.

I had everything I ever wanted.

I had a good job that paid the bills with enough money spare to eat out regularly and go on quarterly holidays in the sun.

I had a four bedroom detached house, a stone's throw from the countryside and just a ten minute drive to the city.

I had a car; I traded it in for a new model every two years. Before it needed an inspection or service, I had a shiny brand new one sitting on my double driveway.

I had a Rottweiler called Buster. Cliché, I know, but he was the final step. The one before you took the plunge and had a baby.

And I had the perfect man. We were happy and we were in love.

See? My life had finally fallen into place.

But little did I know that in my blissful state of ignorance, I was taking everything for granted. I didn't know my time in possession of perfection was running out.

I had no idea I was about to have everything ripped away from me. Again.

I didn't see it coming.

My name is Skye, and this is my story.

***

There has to be a way out. There has to be.

Almost autumn, 2002.

"Skye!"

My mother banged her fist on my bedroom door like she did every morning. Every. Morning.

I groaned and opened my eyes. I was in my third 'snooze' phase of the new day and I was not happy about being woken up before the fourth. Alarm clocks had snooze buttons for a reason.

"Skye!" she called again, and banged. Again. "If I have to listen to that alarm once more, you'll be investing in a new one!"

I groaned again and cursed. I did that a lot at home; I didn't want to be there. I hadn't for a long time; not since my father left to live with his new girlfriend and my life turned to shit. It was a day I would never forget. My mother stood by the kitchen window with her arms folded, looking out at the other houses in the cul-de-sac. My father packed his things and we watched from the sofa as he filled his car and pulled off the driveway. There was no conversation; we didn't get an explanation. He just said goodbye, in a voice that sounded nothing like the one he used when he told us he was proud of us, and he left.

We had a nice house when he lived with us. I had my own room with a big bay window. It's funny how you notice the little things when they're gone.

Living in a family home soon changed. My mother had never had a job and didn't even pretend to try and get one when he walked out. She let the government pay for everything and as a result, we had to move – to a two bedroom flat in a tower block.

It wasn't so bad, if you ignored the pounding music from the neighbours on one side and the suspicious smell of what the couple on the other side were smoking. Oh, and the old lady downstairs. She would bash the ceiling with her broom because she forgot she lived in a third floor flat provided by the council, instead of the bungalow she lived in with her husband before he died. She was nice enough, if you caught her on a good day, when she actually remembered her own name and what year it was.

I didn't hate my father; I didn't blame him for leaving. I only envied him for being able to escape. And I wished he had taken us with him... Us. My twin brother, Oliver, and me. I just wished he had run away with us both in tow.

My mother didn't care that we shared a room. I'm sure, at nineteen, it was illegal. The council didn't care and our mother didn't care enough to try to change it. Beth, our older sister…she got out two years earlier. She moved away to university and apart from the weekly call to make sure we weren't malnourished, she had her own life.

Oliver and I both held down two jobs so we could feed and clothe ourselves, and pay the water rates; we were two showers a day clean freaks. We worked all the hours we could, which was pointless because she only smoked and drank our money away. A vegetable or a hint of colour was a rarity in our fridge.

I was determined to get out, we both were. We decided one night, about five months in when we were high from inhaling next door's fumes,that we wouldn't put up with her for much longer. We would save enough money to move out and get a place together; a place with at least two bedrooms.

We only had each other. We had to stick together; keep each other sane and on the straight and narrow.

"Skye!" My mother's incessant banging and leechy voice continued.

I had turned the damn alarm off ages ago. I realised when she banged again and I considered getting out of bed, opening the door and banging my fist on her face to show her how it felt, that she didn't want me to be late for work. Less money on my paycheck meant fewer Marlboro Lights for her. I would go and earn the money, give her half and not tell her the other half would go into our savings box. Oliver and I would get out soon, I could feel it. Maybe it was the lingering smell of weed from the night before making me delirious, hopeful, when I should have known better than to have hope.

I heaved myself out of bed and looked across the room at my sleeping brother. He had pulled the duvet over his head to block out her voice so he could sleep before work. He had only been home from his other job for a couple of hours.

Marijuana effects or not, I had a feeling we would be okay. I had to keep that energy and channel it into making a better life for us. I could do that. What other choice was there?

But life doesn't work out the way you plan it, no matter how hard you try.

It's the unexpected we all fail to prepare for…

Buy Survival (Twisted #1) on Amazon

Buy Revival (Twisted #2) on Amazon

Buy Thrive (Twisted #3) on Amazon

Connect with Rebecca

Amazon

Facebook

Twitter

Goodreads

Website

Printed in Great Britain
by Amazon.co.uk, Ltd.,
Marston Gate.